WILD GIRLS,
WILD NIGHTS

WILD GIRLS, WILD NIGHTS
TRUE LESBIAN SEX STORIES

Edited by
Sacchi Green

Published in the United States by Cleis Press, Inc., 2246 Sixth Street, Berkeley, California 94710.

Printed in the United States.
Cover design: Scott Idleman/Blink
Cover photograph: Barnaby Hall/Getty Images
Text design: Frank Wiedemann

First Edition.
10 9 8 7 6 5 4 3 2 1

Trade paper ISBN: 978-1-57344-933-5
E-book ISBN: 978-1-57344-950-2

Contents

INTRODUCTION

Writers put themselves into all their work, whether they realize it or not. Even the wildest imagination comes from deep inside. But for this book, I asked them to take a deep breath, go that extra step, and write hot, explicit stories firmly grounded in their personal experience. Real encounters, real emotions, real people with overwhelming desires, drawing on memory rather than imagination to share their own true stories of lesbian sex.

I had no idea who would take up the challenge. Incorporating your memories and longings and secret kinks into fiction is one thing, but putting your name—or a pseudonym your friends may recognize—on a story that exposes intimate, unrestrained details of your life is something else again. Not to mention details of your lovers' lives. I asked that pseudonyms be used for all characters other than the authors, to preserve some degree of privacy. Even so, who was going to open themselves so fearlessly and passionately?

But these authors did, and I'll be forever grateful. Writers have always come through for me, in the course of eight previous anthologies, and they did it again. This time, though, I had the sense that they were also coming through for themselves. The urge to tell their stories was second only to the urgent impulses that drove the action in the first place.

I already knew that truth could be as wild, sensual and searing as any flight of imagination, and these writers went even beyond my hopes. There are stories with spankings, strap-ons, restraints and desert sand; settings ranging from a London hospital to a Caribbean island to Niagara Falls to Tel Aviv; lifetime commitments, fleeting encounters to savor for a lifetime, first flings and at least one threesome. Reality doesn't have to be prosaic. Wet, messy, frenzied, sometimes even awkward, but not boring.

The variety of writers, too, is everything I'd hoped for. Some are well-known and accomplished, telling their tales with skill and artistry that seem to transcend real life, even when they're true. Some are new to writing, experimenting with preserving their treasured experiences in print, while others have been writing for themselves (and each other) for a long time but never dared share their work openly before.

One previously published writer told me that this story felt so personal to her—more than any of her others—that she'd only submit it to an editor and publisher she knows and trusts. Another, new to me, said that writing about her first encounter with a woman excited her all over again. A third described her piece as the true story of a very special event in her own and her partner's lives, with only the names changed to protect the innocence of their grown children (who know she writes but also know her well enough not to want to Google her). I'm always moved, in one sense or another, by the stories people send me, but this time I was touched in a whole new way.

I was also amused by some of the details they shared with me. One said of her story, "All true. I was on Twitter ten minutes later bragging that 'my girlfriend spanked me so hard I cried

real-life tears of ouchiness.' Lots of people were jealous. LOL."
Another, when I asked what she'd been wearing that gave her
partner such easy access, told me that she'd been afraid to admit
at the beginning that she'd stripped to a T-shirt and underpants
right after work, in case it might make her sound silly and too
young, and then she forgot to decide what to say at all. I'm glad
she was much less inhibited about the rest of what happened.

The stories themselves always count most, but in this rare
case a sense of the writer behind each story is important, too.
I've only shared a few of these details, but I've come to know
enough about most of these authors to be confident as to the
basic truth of what they wrote.

The stories can speak for themselves. Some are about first
times, each in a distinctive way, from Angel Propps finding the
leather daddy she hadn't known she needed to Jasmine Grimstead having glorious sex under the stars with the free-spirited
girl of her dreams. Some are inextricably tied to stressful occupa-
tions, like the episode of forbidden lust in the military by Dawn
McKay, and the life-and-death trauma of Lynette Mae's police
work. Many memories are long treasured while some are newly
forged; Catherine Paulssen writes nostalgically of being young in
Germany in the summer of 1994.

Every story deserves special mention, but I've gone on long
enough. Go ahead and enjoy what these women have bravely and
generously offered. With some you'll feel vivid flashbacks to your
own adventures; with others you'll wish you'd shared theirs; and
some will inspire you to make steamy new memories of your
own. Reading these stories to someone with just the same urge
would be a fine way to start.

Sacchi Green
Amherst, MA

POLVO DE HADAS

Monica E. Moreno

When I was fifteen my great-grandmother taught me two things.

The first was that there was magic in the jars she kept on her kitchen counter. Added to the right dish, cinnamon could break a man of his fear of marriage. A few words said over vanilla and marjoram could cure nightmares. Cayenne in the proper amount lit a passion between two lovers that spread as quickly as dandelions over our yard in summer, and then stayed. *Polvo de hadas*, she called these things. Fairy dust.

"Remember this, *m'ija*," she said. "After you forget all the angles they teach you in geometry, you remember this."

The second thing was that I should never make noise during sex. "*Hijas buenas* don't do that, *m'ija*," she told me. Good girls didn't cry out or moan, she insisted.

"Besides," my *bisabuela* said with a wink, her eyelids wrinkled as seashells, "you don't want the boy to think you like it too much, do you? Better to keep him guessing."

And I did remember these things. After I'd forgotten those angles. After a fever came for my ninety-year-old *bisabuela* so quickly she died in her sleep. After I moved my spice jars and everything else I owned into an apartment above a four-washer Laundromat.

I shared those few hundred square feet with a woman who spoke in the tight-jawed almost-drawl of growing up in what my family called a "square state." At twenty-three, Beau had barely a year on me, but it seemed like an infinite distance. Her long silences thrilled and terrified me. If a hair crack appeared at the edge of our bathtub, she had it caulked before I could mention it over breakfast. She owned three pairs of shoes to my fifteen, and lived in jeans and plaid flannel. Barely five-two, she held herself like a man a foot taller, and stood shy but settled in a boyish body, save for the wide hips she hid in Levi's 501s.

Beau always looked that way, stolid and sure, so I didn't know she was a virgin until the first night I tugged off her doubled-up undershirts and spread my hands over her back. Her fingers, clumsy for once, pulled my panties aside, fidgeting with the lace and not certain about what to do next. She didn't know it was my first time either. She figured from my lipsticks and ruffled skirts and how quickly I'd said yes to moving in with her that I must've done it at least once, maybe under wooden bleachers or on a dew-wet soccer field in high school.

We laughed in the dark when we realized, both nervous that there was no one who knew the way enough to lead. But we learned.

Aside from that laughing, I never made noise during sex, sure my great-grandmother's warnings held for a girl who looked so much like a boy. My collarbone trembled against Beau's shoulder, but I always held my lips together to stop the sound. She'd press her body into mine, my heart flinching at her weight and heat and the way she still pulled my panties aside, too impatient to take them off. I stayed quiet, biting her shoulder to make sure I didn't scream.

It was why I never let her use her mouth on me, because I knew I'd break that essential silence if I felt the warmth and wetness of her tongue there. Instead, I did it to her, moving my lips against her and getting drunk off how her scent caught in the hair between her legs. But I never asked her for the same, and never let her. She'd try once a month or so, giving her cowboy's nod and saying she'd like to "know what it's like down there." I'd shrug her off with a red lipstick-kiss on her back and a whisper about how I liked giving better than receiving.

"How d'ya know if you've never received?" Beau asked every time, but every time I ignored her.

It was around that time that I realized I wanted Beau in my bed forever. I didn't care if we spent the next sixty years in that four-hundred-square-foot apartment, the smell of a dozen different detergents and fabric softeners wafting up from the Laundromat. I didn't care if I startled awake every morning at the sound of quarters turning over in the coin return downstairs. I didn't even mind the shrieking on Saturday nights, when a group of dental hygienists from down the street came in so drunk on apple martinis they brought dishwashing powder instead of detergent.

And if I wanted Beau, for good, I'd need my *bisabuela*'s cinnamon and cayenne.

The cinnamon was easy. I added a teaspoon to coffee grounds in the morning, and Beau only noticed enough to ask, "D'you do something different? I like it." I shook a little more cinnamon than I needed to into apple muffin batter. I even made my great-grandmother's *mole negro*, grinding *cacao* and black walnuts in a mortar because our apartment didn't have the room for a *comal.* While the *mole* simmered, I added so much cinnamon that I could almost hear my *bisabuela* clucking her tongue. "That much, *m'ija*? She'll get you a ring by Pentecost."

That left the cayenne. Cayenne wouldn't slide into dishes the way cinnamon did. Cinnamon added warmth and woodiness but not shouting its presence. Cayenne, however, meant business. If I ever added enough to make a difference, Beau would know, and she wouldn't like it. She never went in for spice. Not *poblanos*, not chili powder, not even the bell peppers that were sweet more than spicy but that she swore had "a kick to 'em." My corn and jalapeno salsa almost choked her, and if I wanted to add red chili flakes to a shared order of French fries, I had to keep them on my side.

"Some *gringos*, they have tongues tame as rabbits," my great-grandmother had told me once. "They're sensitive. They taste everything."

Remembering that made me even surer that I'd never let Beau's tongue between my legs. What if I'd eaten so many peppers since I was a little girl that every part of me had turned spicy? What if the place between my thighs tasted hot and tart as chili oil? My *gringo* might try me once and decide not only that she never wanted that dish again, but that she wanted a different menu, a different kitchen, a different girl.

Beau was all rock salt and green herbs. She knew tarragon and onion powder at least, two staples of her family's recipes, but her home county had taught her plain meat-and-potatoes. It was only by the grace of her mother's herb garden that she never questioned all the green things I kept in little glass jars and added to dinner every night.

All I could do was get her used to my *polvo de hadas*, hope she'd warm up to it. Each night during dinner I left a little bowl of cayenne out on the table between us, the powder bright as marigolds against ceramic the color of peacock's down. I learned my aunts' recipes for *enchiladas de calabaza* and blue corn *tamales*, things that begged for a sprinkle of heat and orange-red as deep as sundown. Beau never touched the cayenne. I made *frijoles* so underseasoned I was sure she'd throw on anything within reach. She only added a dash of salt and told me she liked when I made her things from my family, and would I let her make me a few plates she grew up with once her work shifts let up next week.

A few nights later, I pushed the turquoise ceramic toward her, and she nudged it back, telling me, "That's your stuff. You need it near you. You use it like salt."

I edged it toward her plate again. "Try it," I said, sounding like my aunts coaxing my cousins into sipping *atole* for the first time.

Beau shrugged, and didn't.

I pushed my half-eaten *tlayuda* away, got up from the table and scrubbed at the oiled pan in the sink.

Beau stood behind me and held my waist, the flannel of her shirt sleeves warming the band of skin between my blouse and my skirt. "Hey," she said, in the soft, low voice I imagined got her near the elk that crossed her family's land. "What's the matter?"

I took the steel wool to the film of canola, spraying us both with a fine mist of dishwater. "Nothing."

She held my waist tighter. "Tell me."

I tried shaking her, but she spread her hands. Her fingers hooked into the ribbon that tied my skirt closed.

She laughed. "Is it 'cause I won't put chili powder on my dinner?"

I gave up on the pan and moved to the knives I'd used for the lettuce and tomatillos.

"I've tried it before," Beau said. "Never liked it."

I turned around, not breaking her hold on my waist. I shifted in her arms until my breasts, buoyed by the lace of my bra, pressed against hers, bound flat by the two cotton undershirts she wore beneath the plaid flannel.

"What's the matter?" I tapped a finger under her chin, leaving a clover flower of soap bubbles on her jawline. "Can't take the heat?"

She shrugged again, one shoulder, bowing her head so her hair fell in her eyes. "Maybe."

I cleared the bloom of little bubbles with my thumb. The dish soap left behind the scent of citrus or water lilies or whatever she picked up the week before, whatever was on special.

"How come you need me to so bad?" Beau asked.

"I don't," I said.

She said my name, pressing her hand into the small of my back. The sweat from her palm made the muscles in my thighs tense.

"You have to or it won't work," I said.

"What won't work?" she asked.

"It's magic. *Polvo de hadas*."

"*Polvo de* what?" she asked.

"Fairy dust." I studied the linoleum between our feet, mine bare, hers in the soft cotton of tube socks. "To get you to fall in love with me."

Another slice of her hair fell in front of her right eye. "Don't need fairy dust for that."

I met her eyes, the black centers still as river rocks.

"Really?" I asked.

"Too late anyway." Her fingers caught in the loops of the bow on my skirt. "You gotta know that by now."

I looked over at the table, the little bowl of cayenne still in the center of the wood. "But could it hurt?"

She laughed. "Look, you want me to do something for you, you gotta do something for me."

"What?" I asked.

"You trust me?"

"Yes."

"So if I let you give me your fairy dust, you'll do something for me?"

"Like what?"

"No questions," she said. "Just yes or no."

"Yes," I said, not looking back at the turquoise ceramic that held my great-grandmother's *polvo de hadas*.

"All right then," Beau said, her weight so settled in her lower body that I startled when she gripped my waist. She took me the little distance across our tiny kitchen and lifted me onto the wooden table, pushing our plates aside along with that blue bowl. With one hand catching the weight of my head and neck, she lowered me to lying down and then climbed on top of me. The old wooden table rattled but held steady. Beau's denim and flannel covered me as she put her mouth to mine.

The taste of tomatillos had turned sweet in her mouth, like blood oranges. She kissed me harder, her fingers pulling the ribbon on my skirt loose. I was ready, even if the table turned to splinters and scrap wood under our weight. My upper back arched off the table as Beau pushed up my skirt and pulled my panties aside.

I didn't realize what she was doing until I felt not her fingers but the heat of her tongue between my legs. It spread wetness as thick as the syrup of *los helechos culantrillos*. I screamed in surprise, in protest as halfhearted as it was momentary. Her tongue sent pleasure through me so hard and so quickly I was sure she was kissing a place I had never found with my hands.

Each time I moved, her mouth pursued me, easing my mouth open to let the sound out.

Then I remembered what my *bisabuela* told me, and I dug my teeth into my lower lip to keep myself quiet.

Beau came up for air, her lips shining wet. "Don't stop," she said, the same words that were on my lips. But I couldn't give them sound. I couldn't let my lips make any noise or I would scream again, the way *una hija buena* never would.

"Don't stop," Beau said again.

With the same half smile I'd seen every time she caught me just out of the shower, soaked and dripping, Beau took a pinch of cayenne from the turquoise bowl and sprinkled it over each of my thighs. A little of it swirled in the air, drifting like snow.

"Beau." I squirmed and laughed, the spice tingling on my skin, making me wetter and sensitive as my breasts after a hot bath. "Beau," I said, laughing at the feeling of her hands on my sides. "What are you doing?"

She took as much from the bowl as she could pinch between two fingers and let it fall like snow over me. It dusted the wood of the table. It frosted the hair between my legs red so it looked like threads of saffron.

"You want your fairy dust in me," Beau said. "Then I wanna get in you."

She lowered her mouth to my panties and licked away every constellation of the *polvo de hadas*. Her tongue lapped at my thighs like the first brazen waves of a tide coming in. Her mouth kissed the place I had never let her kiss with such hunger I was sure she thought it would kiss back. She set her teeth at the pain of the unfamiliar spice on her tongue and the rapture of being somewhere I had never allowed her. Her tongue circled the most sensitive point on me, and a scream opened my mouth.

Beau did not let me into the button fly of her jeans until she had found each grain on my damp skin. And when she kissed me long after midnight, the heat of the cayenne still clung to her lips, passing the dark magic and beautiful sting of the *polvo de hadas* from her mouth to mine. I looked through the screen of my eyelashes, my hair trailing off the edge of the table, and I could see cinnamon shimmering in the air.

HOT DESERT NIGHTS

Dawn McKay

They tell you about the heat of the desert, and the sand. God, how I hate the sand. It was 2005 and we were deep in the heart of Don't Ask, Don't Tell, military-speak for *gay is a dirty secret.*

I was three months into a six-month deployment when all hell broke loose. Casualties were incoming, and my section had been activated as manpower to move patients from the choppers to the hospital. All the practice in the world can't prepare you for what you see. I know. I'll never forget it.

An hour in, and my mind grew numb. Tears had long since dried on my face. My arms were still strong, responding auto-matically to my lift partners.

Three hours in, and I didn't even remember my name. I was reaching for the next wounded soldier in the Black Hawk when a hand touched my forearm. I looked up into the most beautiful green eyes I'd ever seen. She struck me as a fairy, cute pert nose, short-cropped sable hair, jade green eyes and a smile that nearly knocked me on my ass. She was stunning. "Hang in there" was all she said, but it was enough. I nodded abruptly, gave a small smile and pulled the next patient. Throughout the afternoon I saw her half a dozen times and caught myself looking for her, wishing for that smile to keep me going. I'd noticed she was a captain, so definitely untouchable, but I wanted to get to know her, see that smile to fight off the worst of my day.

After twelve hours we were finally done. The patients were stabilized, settled down for the night or in the air to Germany. We were released back to our tents for much-needed showers. I was returning from my cleansing and debating hanging with the guys. In my heart I knew they'd laugh off the day and do whatever they could to ignore the horrors we'd seen. I just couldn't face it. So I turned to my tent—and there she was, standing at the flap of my door with her hands behind her back, in a fresh flight suit, smiling. The suit hugged her curves like a second skin. She was damned lovely. I had to be dreaming. My nipples hardened, and I was thankful for the sports bra that covered them.

"Hey. Remember me?" Her voice was low, a sexy rumble I really liked.

"Hey yourself." I smiled the first genuine smile since the nightmare began. The towel hung around my neck, and I tugged on it to hide my shyness. "You're not easy to forget." My cheeks heated with embarrassment.

She blushed, and I had a moment of uncertainty. We both knew what could happen from her being at my tent in the first place. Officer and enlisted unprofessional relationships were forbidden and grounds for dismissal from the service, never mind the thoughts that were running around in my head.

"How did you find me?"

She chuckled. "I'm a flight surgeon. All I had to do was chitchat with my people here, and ask the right kind of questions."

"Ahh" was all I could think to say.

She cleared her throat and smiled. "The name's Holly." She held up a few minibar bottles of Jack. "I thought you could use a stiff one."

I grinned. "Dawn. Nice to put a name to the face." Skulking around in the dark with alcohol in a dry deployment, and sharing with an enlisted person? This woman was insane. I stepped close enough that I could smell the freshness of soap and the strong floral scent of her shampoo. With a flourish and a tiny bow, I opened my tent flap. "Welcome to my humble home." Hell, even if all we did was talk, it would be better than staying alone with my thoughts. And the nightmares to come.

She ducked in and looked around. "You have roommates?" Two other beds were in the small tent.

"They're all mids. Won't be back until six in the morning." Five hours. A lot could happen in five hours.

She stood in the middle of my tent, turned and dropped a well-worn backpack at her feet. Tension mounted between us. I gripped the towel with tight fists.

"I don't want to be alone tonight." She said the words quietly.

"Neither do I." I had to be dreaming. This couldn't be happening.

She walked up to me, slim, beautiful and taller than me by a few inches. "I could get decommissioned for having alcohol here."

I smiled. "You could. And I could lose a stripe for taking it from you."

She grinned and handed me a bottle. I wasn't a fan of the whiskey, but after this day, I needed the shield of alcohol. The Jack hurt going down, but not as much as the memory of the day did. She downed a bottle, gently took mine from my fingers and slipped them back into her backpack. I knew she had more, but I wanted a clear head for the next day.

"Why are you here?" I wanted it out in the open. No surprises. No misunderstandings. No drama.

"The crew was grounded for the night. The pilot had too many hours in the air."

I smiled, brushing her cheek with the back of my knuckles, pushing back a stray hair that had slipped down. "That's not what I meant." My hand fell away, back to the towel.

Holly cupped my face with trembling hands and brushed her lips over mine. A flare of heat shot down to my core. This was going to be interesting. It had been almost five months since I'd had anything but my own fingers seeing to my satisfaction. I closed my eyes for a brief instant, and she pulled away just enough to look me in the eyes as they opened. "I want you." Her voice shook. "The moment I saw you, I wanted you. I looked for you every time we landed, and couldn't get you off my mind." She seemed confused by that. I could definitely sympathize.

"Your smile got me through the day." I smiled at her, a gentle sad tilt to my lips. My thoughts were returning to the day, to the mess of bodies, the cries of pain. It was tearing me apart.

Soft lips were on mine, tasting, sampling. I melted into it, latching on to something solid. My hands cupped her cheeks, and I brushed my tongue against her lips in gentle swipes. Her mouth opened and my tongue delved into the warm depths. She tasted like Jack and strawberry candy. A strange combination. My fingers traced the line of her jaw, the slope of her shoulder. Irritated by the barrier of her flight suit, I dragged down the zipper. Her gasp of surprise was followed by a sharp tug of my hair and sexy nips at my throat. A spike of pleasure shot down my spine; I love having my hair tugged. Her tongue and mouth teased a line down my neck, sending soft shivers of delight racing down my body, to my nipples, my pussy. I wanted this woman. Really wanted her.

I slipped my fingers under the collar of the flight suit, caressing her shoulders, scraping my nails lightly against her throat. She kissed her way down to the collar of my shirt and gave a sexy growl that shot my excitement that much higher.

"There's going to be a windstorm tonight. I heard the tower talking about it." She spoke the words against my throat. Windstorms meant no one would be out and the enemy would be sending mortar attacks.

"Off." She tugged at my shirt.

I backed away, holding up my hands to stave off her question. "Hold that thought." I went to the tent door and zipped it shut, then unrolled the second layer, shower curtains. Hey, you make do with what you have. Stones held them down, trapping most of the dust that would attempt to tear through the small holes at the door. It wasn't perfect, but it was effective.

Her arms came around from behind me, tugging my body against hers. I could feel her breasts pressed against my back. She was soft, yet strong. I reached up and touched her head, pressing it against mine. My other hand settled on her arms. A quiet moment—but we both wanted more.

I turned around in the circle of her arms and kissed her, dragging the zipper of her flight suit all the way past her belly button. My hands slid back up. Her skin was soft. I loved how her stomach tightened at my touch, how her breathing quickened. My fingers slipped past the dog tags around her throat. She opened my uniform shirt, cleverly tugging gently to pull the buttons loose. My towel dropped on the bed, forgotten. Her hands slid under the shirt, pushing it down my arms. My T-shirt followed. She tossed them both on a chair and stepped back, dragging her uniform off. I sat on the chair and unlaced my boots, admiring the glow of her skin, and yet wishing I had a cute little body like hers. I love the way a woman is built.

The rest of my uniform came off in a rush, and I stood and strode toward her. She held up her hands, and I stopped. With a sexy little shimmy, Holly unlatched her bra, letting it slide off her arms. Pert breasts with rose-colored, hard nipples. Her panties followed, and I was surprised to note her pussy was hairless.

My panties and bra came off. I wasn't hairless, but I was trimmed. The heat of the desert demanded it.

"You are beautiful." Her breathless compliment made my cheeks hot. I held out my hand and she walked to me, slipping her hand into mine.

"You are gorgeous." She was. Truly gorgeous. What the hell was she doing with me? I tugged her against my body. Soft skin to soft skin. There is nothing like a woman's body against yours. So soft, yet fit, curves to die for. I love women in all sizes. The kiss we shared fired my blood, making my pussy clench in excited anticipation. Part of me expected her to change her mind, realize how crazy this was, how insane we had to be.

We lay on the bed. The mattress was small, but we fit closely, and it beat the hell out of the cots we'd had a couple of months ago. I explored Holly's body with delicate care, teasing over her nipples, lightly caressing, then pinching, loving the soft groans from her throat as they tightened to hard points.

Each kiss was near desperation. My ears were constantly open to movement outside the tent. The threat of being caught sent my lust higher, deepening my need. Her nails traced over my body, driving me insane with her teasing strokes. She found a spot on my hip that sent chills of lust all over my body. Her luscious mouth explored from the curve of my neck down my chest, then covered my nipple, and her teeth tugged delicately. I moaned. My fingers teased her pussy, swirling around her slit. She arched against my touch, and I let a finger slip in. She clenched around my finger, and I moaned. "What a sweet pussy." I flicked my finger.

Holly's soft cry was swallowed by my lips. She tugged my hair, and her kiss turned desperate. She was nearly dripping with her desire. I stroked and teased, wanting to send her higher. My fingers rubbed her moist essence around her clit. A clit I wanted to torment and tease just to hear her cries. Another finger slipped in, stroking. "So hot, Holly. Is this all for me?"

"Yes." She arched against me, fucking my fingers. "All of it. I want you to use all of it." I raised my eyebrows. My fist? She must have seen the confusion on my face. A smile slipped across her lips and she lifted up. "Like this." She took my hand and arranged the fingers in a tapered formation.

"Do you have any kind of lube?" Her question was breathless.

"Just some baby oil in the toiletry bag hanging up beside you."

She grabbed the bottle and grinned, pouring oil on my hand, getting it nice and ready, then rubbing it around and into her pussy. I was terrified I would hurt her. At the same time, there was a craving to be in control, to give her what she needed. My hands were small, but I had no idea what I was doing. What if I hurt her somehow? I could taste her excitement in the air, feel her need like it was my own. The bottle went back in the bag, and she wiped her fingers on the towel.

"Tell me if I hurt you." My experiences were limited, especially since I joined the service.

She ran her fingers along my cheek. A soft kiss from my lips to hers, and she lay back, spreading wide for me. She was a sight.

A desert goddess. My memory may be jaded, but she brought a miracle to me that night.

I pressed, gently, spreading her sweet pussy. I watched the lips fold open like a flower, and dewy essence slipped around my fingers. My arms were sore and stiff from the day's work, but I didn't want to stop for anything. My hand began a light thrust, slipping deeper into her pussy with every stroke. Holly arched and groaned in obvious pleasure. I stroked deeper, and she bit her lip to stifle a loud groan. Her inner muscles tightened around me. It was like nothing I'd ever felt before.

Sex, baby oil, and Holly's unique scent mixed together, so hot I could almost taste it. My pace increased and Holly lifted her ass off the bed to fuck my hand in near desperation.

"It won't take long," she gasped, frantically rubbing her clit.

My arm shook from the efforts, and I was afraid I wouldn't be able to keep going.

Holly yanked my pillow from under her head and pressed it to her face, muffling her cries. Her inner muscles rippled and tightened, pulsing against my hand. Finally her body relaxed, and she slowly lowered her hips back to the tangled sheets. Tiny tremors squeezed around my hand. I slowly withdrew, gently caressing her pussy lips with shaking fingers.

The wind picked up and my door flapped slightly. My heart still raced, thundering with the storm. Holly tugged my fingers away from her pussy and brought them to my lips. She spread her juices across my bottom lip and then leaned forward, kissing me, sucking her juice from me. I moaned. My pussy ached for her touch.

She pulled away from the kiss and slipped off the bed. I could see the same hunger in her face. She grabbed my hips and tugged me to the edge of the bed. I gripped the towel in the hand

I'd fucked Holly with. In a heartbeat she had my thighs spread, her gaze hot on my body, like a heavy caress. "Let's see if you taste as good as you smell." Holly put a hand on my chest and pushed, gently knocking me back against the mattress.

She held my lips open. Her breath blew across my clit, warm and sexy. Her tongue swiped at my clit. Sharp pleasure shot to my core, and my inner muscles tightened. She licked and sucked, driving me insane with her clever mouth. She tongue-fucked my pussy with rapid flicks. Wind battered against the tent, and the storm grew outside, and inside my body as well.

I arched against her, begging, pleading for release. Her tongue was incredible, but I needed more. I slipped my hands down to my pussy, tightly holding my lips open.

"Thank you." Her words brushed against my skin.

Any comment I would have made spun away when two fingers thrust deep into my pussy. I arched against her touch. Her tongue lapped and flicked. Pleasure built at the base of my spine, waiting for the right combination of pressure and stimulation. It had been too long. She sucked my clit, and I came apart. I think I might have shouted. For the first time since I'd arrived, I was thankful for a sandstorm. Sparks lit behind my eyelids, and I twitched with mini-aftershocks. She swiped her tongue once more against my pussy, then withdrew her fingers. I sat up and drew her quickly to me. She had a self-satisfied grin on her face. I'd give her that. My lips twitched in an answering smile, and I just held her hands while she stood between my legs on the bed. I let go to caress her face with my clean hand, brushing my fingers against her temple. She grabbed my hand and turned to place a kiss on the palm. Her eyes were closed, and I knew what was coming next.

Some unknown emotion, close to regret, tightened in my chest.

I brushed my thumb against her face and gently turned her cheek. She opened her eyes and I was once again taken by the incredible color and emotion staring back at me.

I pulled her in for a soft kiss. My scent and taste blended with the unique flavor of Holly, a flavor I'd never forget. Our lips touched with tender, sweet caresses. I savored the touch of her tongue against mine, until we parted with regret.

"I'll see you around," she said.

"Yeah." I knew I wouldn't. So did she.

"I need to go before the morning." Her voice was quiet, low and sad.

I wanted to tell her to wait until the sandstorm was over. Tell her the hell with regulations and stay with me. But I wouldn't.

"I know you do." I grabbed her hands and squeezed them. "It's okay." It really was. I knew when this started what it would be.

We quietly got dressed, she in her flight suit, I in a fresh T-shirt and panties. I gently wiped her face and hands with moist towelettes, cleaning away all proof of what we'd done. She pulled a Jolly Rancher out of one of her numerous pockets, unwrapped it and popped it in her mouth. Strawberry.

My arms trembled as I hugged her one last time. I told myself it was from all the heavy lifting earlier. Her smile was still as beautiful as before. She left as quietly as she had come, slipping from my tent in the middle of a sandstorm.

I cleaned myself up with quiet efficiency and then, with a sigh, lay down on my bed and stared at the hanging ceiling. The sound of mortar fire powered through the storm. They were at it again. I held my dog tags, tugging on the chain so that it rested between my breasts, and drifted to sleep dreaming of jade green eyes and an amazing smile. The brightest spot in the next three months of hell. I'll never forget her.

THE DADDY
I DIDN'T KNOW
I NEEDED

Angel Propps

I could hear the loud rumble and purr of the motorcycle long before it roared into the nearly empty lot of the diner where I waitressed. My heart began to pound so hard it felt like I was about to be a victim of a heart attack. When I looked down I could see a pulsing beat just below the flesh.

The reason for my nervousness came walking through the door, bringing the smell of cigarettes and gasoline with her. I waited behind the counter, wiping at the same few inches of grease-covered chrome with the dish towel and praying that she would sit at my station. She usually did, but I was always terrified that she wouldn't. I was equally terrified that she would. That night she did.

She didn't look like other women I knew; she looked hard and tough. Her body was muscular and thick, her hair stood up in sooty black points and her shoulders were broad under the leather jacket she always wore. To stop looking at her shoulders I always dropped my eyes, and inevitably they fell to the long silver chain that swung across her hip from one belt loop to her back pocket. I knew her wallet resided in that pocket, and something about that fact made my crotch throb—why, I could not have said.

I poured her coffee, then looked at her and asked, "Would you like to go out with me?"

She sat there, a sugar packet caught between her fingers and her dark brown eyes open wide. The cook was whistling in the kitchen behind me, the only other customer in the place sat at the far end of the counter noisily working his way through chocolate cream pie and Tammy, my fellow waitress, stood in the parking lot chain-smoking Kools. Everything was normal but totally upside down.

"Listen"—her eyes flickered against the name tag on my wilted pink uniform—"Angel. I do not need some asshole screwing with me. I come in here to eat, not be the butt of your little joke."

"I wasn't joking," I got out. "I'm off work. I was just hanging around to see if you wanted to go somewhere a little quieter."

"Is this a new twist on the coffee, tea or me trick?"

I could not even answer that because my nerve totally failed me. I grabbed my purse and bolted through the glass doors so hard that I literally ejected myself out of the bright diner and into the dark parking lot. I was angry at myself for asking and even angrier at her for rejecting me.

"Wait!" she called.

I turned around and opened my mouth to tell her to go fuck herself, but the sight of the bulge near her crotch made me close my mouth.

"I'm going home. If you want, you can follow me there."

There was a major dare in her words and I knew it. What was more, I wanted to take that dare. I wanted to be alone with her.

"See you there," I said, and got into my car while she walked to her bike.

Following her, I was so nervous I kept accidentally speeding up and almost running her over; once she stopped at a light and held a hand up over her head in a gesture of surrender that made me laugh even as I jerked to a halt.

She pulled into the driveway of a shabby little house and killed her headlight. I parked along the curb and got out of my car. The sound of my door shutting seemed very loud and I glanced around nervously at the darkened houses that sat on the quiet street, wondering if the neighbors could see me. She walked toward the door and I followed her, mostly because I had no idea what else to do.

I stood in her living room, watching her light incense cones and open two cans of beer. My arms broke out in a rash of goose pimples and my pussy felt heavy, full. There was an uncomfortable amount of wetness in my panties and tears building in my eyes. I didn't know what to say, so I blurted out the first thing that came to mind.

"I don't know your name."

"I'm Sam."

I reached out one finger to touch her hair. I had to touch it. I had to feel those sharp points of hair under my fingers. And that was all it took.

Her mouth came down on mine. Our tongues moved together and apart, our breath mingled and when her hands ran down the curve of my spine and tilted my crotch into hers, I moaned into her mouth in pure surrender.

She guided me down the hallway and into a dark bedroom. Her mouth kept coming back to mine while she stripped me bare. My ugly pink uniform made a soft sighing sound as it hit the floor. I shook all over. My arms crossed over my tits and I felt my toes curling into the thin carpet. I stiffened with fear when her fingers slid into the hair that covered my wet pink pussy lips, and then relaxed as she stroked and caressed me.

I thought I was going to fall down. My legs were trembling and I couldn't breathe. Sweat trickled down my neck and crept from under my hairline. My hips jerked forward once, a silent plea that she understood perfectly.

Sam laid me down in her bed. It creaked as she knelt between my legs and asked, "Do you trust me?"

"Yes."

I did. For no reason I could think of I trusted her, and for a long moment there was only her breath blowing across my neck. Then her tongue flicked out and across my nipples. They tightened instantly, painfully. The reaction shocked me. My eyes squeezed shut as her mouth encircled one of those nipples and tugged at it. Teeth teased and her tongue soothed the pain those teeth left behind. I started to cry.

Sam's mouth went lower. Sensation came and went. I cried out again and again long before she took pity on me. Her fingers parted my labia, her tongue darted in and I let out a small shriek. Her fingers stroked my clit and then she spread my legs wider, bending them and pushing them upward.

The wetness had become unbearable. She spread it across my tender skin between my pussy and asshole and blew on it. Her breath tingled against that slippery oil, my hips arched instinctively and she chuckled. Her tongue flickered across my clit, then she nipped at it. One of her thick fingers probed my pussy and I fucked it, trying desperately to match her rhythm. She added another finger, then another, until I felt stretched wide, but I still wanted more. A finger probed at my asshole while others slid in and out of my cunt. The friction began to blur, and I lost the ability to know exactly where her fingers were inside me.

Her tongue was insistent; it licked and tickled at my clit, causing hot squirmy sensations deep inside my gut.

"Do you want to come?"

I answered her with a sobbed-out yes.

"Then come for me, pretty girl," she growled against my aching clit, and I found myself thrusting harder and faster, trying to take everything she was giving.

There was a moment when I strained as hard as I could; then my pussy began to spasm and shudder, my legs shook and my back twisted into a question mark shape. My fingers dug more deeply into her scalp and I could hear the noises I was making but could not stop them.

Sam had taken her jeans off but still wore a T-shirt and boxer shorts. The ivory of those shorts drew my eye as she reached inside the slit and pulled the cock through it, hefting it in her hand. It was thick and long, jutting out from her body like it belonged there.

She positioned herself on her knees and forearms. The bed sagged under her weight and the smooth head of her cock rubbed against my pussy lips. She put a bare inch of it inside me, then withdrew, smirking when I started to arch upward, trying to get that cock all the way inside me. She thrust hard and fast, a quick and ruthless movement that filled me up, and I moaned, my hands clenching into fists.

"Wrap your legs around me," Sam said in my ear, and I did. Under my heels her T-shirt-clad back felt solid and warm. I closed my eyes, letting her take me with her as she fucked me slow and easy, opening me up and allowing her own pleasure to grow.

"That's right, that's a good girl. Let Daddy have it, baby."

The words made my eyes open and for one moment a terrible sense of shame crashed over me. Then I saw her face. Her eyelids were at half-mast and her upper teeth were biting into her lower lip so hard they looked driven into the flesh. Her cheeks were suffused with crimson and her nostrils were flared. It was the sexiest fucking thing I had ever seen and I forgot everything else.

Her body was heavy but the weight was comforting. Her hips slammed into mine and her hands slid beneath me, lifting me onto her cock, and I found that she had not been giving me all of it after all. The friction came back, my pussy ran and I began to whimper and moan.

"That's right, baby girl, let Daddy make you come again. Let Daddy give you something sweet."

"Daddy," I cried, "Daddy, please let me come again!"

The word *Daddy* had a familiar shape on my tongue, but not in my head, and for one second I was sure I was going to hell—and then I came. Come spurted out of me and onto her cock and cotton-clad thighs.

"Hold still," Sam said.

Her hands pressed my hips into the mattress and her chin dug into my shoulder. Her hips were moving so hard that the headboard of the bed crashed into the wall, making a heavy thump with every single thrust.

"I want to fuck you so hard," she panted out. "I want to be so fucking deep inside you."

I felt confused at that—she *was* fucking me hard, she *was* inside me. I couldn't think, I could barely breathe. There was something so primitive about being held down, being helpless and having her fuck me that way.

"I'm going to come inside your pussy," Sam said and her hands came up off my hips and squeezed my shoulders so hard that I cried out in pain even as she collapsed on top of me.

Long minutes ticked by. I counted the time in heartbeats.

I was warm and sleepy under her weight and I could feel little trickles of her breath stirring my hair. One part of me wanted to ask why she had said she was going to come inside me, another part of me knew that to ask would be wrong. I had never had a woman say that to me before, and between that and the fact that I had called her Daddy, I was torn between feeling sexy and feeling uncomfortable.

She rolled us over so that we were facing each other. I could smell her sweat and the scent of sex and cigarettes.

"That was nice," I said finally and Sam howled with laughter.

"I'm glad you think so."

"Why didn't you take off your clothes?"

Her face lost its cocky smug expression. Her features went smooth but there was wariness in her eyes.

"I'm stone."

"What?"

"If you come back we'll talk about it then."

I decided to leave it alone. The whole thing was beginning to feel utterly surreal. I knew I was going to have to deal with all of it, but right then all I wanted was to lie there and feel her body heat.

"Will you come back?"

"Yeah," I whispered.

"Good. You need a Daddy, little girl."

I didn't know what to say to that except that I had to go home. She smoked cigarette after cigarette while I washed and dressed. She walked me to my car and opened the door for me. I had never had that done for me before, and I stood there feeling awkward because I was unsure of how to get in with her standing there.

Driving home I could feel the imprint of her hands on my

hips and shoulders, feel an aching in my pussy that was as plea-surable as it was painful.

"You needed a Daddy, little girl," I said to the pale-faced woman in my rearview mirror, and then I burst into laughter. "And you didn't even know."

"I know now," the woman in my rearview returned.

A few nights later I pulled my car up in front of Sam's house, got out and stood there wondering if she had really wanted me to come back.

Her front door opened and she stepped out onto the front step.

"Are you coming inside, little girl?" she called.

"Yes, Daddy," I called back, and went across the grass to meet her.

THE CORRUPTION OF THE INNOCENT PORNOGRAPHER

Destiny Moon

When asked what she wanted for Christmas, my lover told me she wanted an *experience*. She didn't need any *things*, she emphasized. It's true. She is a minimalist. She has that perfect butch bathroom equipped with a bar of soap, a toothbrush, natural toothpaste and unscented lotion. She is still using the same bottle of shampoo she was using when we first started dating almost one year ago.

Even though my own bathroom is full of products and scented delights, I never want to change anything about her. She's the yin to my yang.

It only took a couple of clicks online to find an experience I was quite sure she would treasure: a stay at a bed & breakfast called the Chocolate Suite run by a couple of passionate chocolatiers who make organic chocolate from scratch. In addition to their chocolate shop storefront, they created the ultimate lesbian fantasy—a private resort where the décor is chocolate brown and the shelves are lined with chocolate-themed movies

and books. Guests also get a complimentary box of chocolates.
I was sold. I booked it and then I proudly announced—in the
first week of December—that my Christmas shopping was officially done.

That was not entirely true because I still needed to buy
beeswax candles, new lingerie, massage oil and wrist restraints.
All month, she was tortured and wanted to know what treat
I was preparing for her. I told her she was in control and if
she really wanted to know, all she had to do was ask and I'd
tell her. The traditionalist in her couldn't stand the thought of
finding out before Christmas morning so, like a good bottom,
she waited patiently.

Meanwhile, I plotted. I planned. I turned myself on thinking
about everything I was going to surprise her with. Semi-frus-
trated, I masturbated. No amount of solo climaxing equaled the
pleasure that I craved. Throughout December, we maintained
our scheduled dates. We had the same stellar sex we always
have. But secretly, I longed to take us in a new direction.

Before I go on, I need to back up. To fully appreciate the
events that took place at the Chocolate Suite, it is important
to understand a few things about my lover. The first thing is
that she is a pornographer. She documents lesbian sex and, as
a natural spin-off of filming lesbian sex as a business, she also
starred in a number of lesbian porn movies, some of her own
design and some directed by others. In other words, she knows
lesbian sex. She has seen a lot and had a lot. She has a massive
circle of fans. She's one of those people who make regular
appearances on lists of hot lesbians.

When that was all I knew about her, I wasn't that interested
in dating her. I didn't want to be with a "hot lesbian" if she had
the ego of one, so I spent a long time ignoring her advances. In
fact, for half a year, I only saw her to work out. We'd walk or

go to the gym and whenever she suggested something beyond that, I said no.

I had yet to learn the other things about her, the things that make her who she is—the woman I love. She grew up in a small prairie town. Her mother is a minister. She went to Bible camp throughout her youth and she's still deeply spiritual. In addition to being a lesbian sex symbol, she is also painfully shy. She is more of a voyeur than an exhibitionist.

One day, while we were out for a walk, a couple of months before we started dating, she confessed something to me. She told me she is vanilla. I paused. I looked at her. I shook my head. She had just come back from a play party she helped to organize in a different city.

"People don't believe me," she pleaded.

"Of course they don't," I said.

After that, we processed the stuff she had witnessed at the party, things she said she didn't understand. Poor dear.

"My business is lesbian sex. I'm in those circles. People just assume I'm kinky and that I've tried everything, but I'm not and I haven't."

I didn't know why she was divulging this to me, but I found it fascinating and encouraged her to tell me more. As her workout partner, I found out about her previous relationships and her favorite and least favorite sexual memories. We talked in ways that only workout partners can—panting and sweating up and down hills and pathways without any sexual stimulation. At the time, I was celibate and single and consciously so. I had ended several overlapping poly relationships that called for a pause. I was in a time of self-reflection. I was more than happy to listen to other people's sex stories, especially hers.

She became a curious oddity to me, like Bettie Page. Even though Bettie Page became the poster girl of early kink portraiture, she maintained a certain naïve quality, like she never really knew why others found her sexually attractive. In her later years, she gave it all up and went back to the church to live a quiet, humble life of worship and fellowship. Though I and her many fans miss her, I respect her ability to walk away and recreate herself.

Time passed, and eventually I said yes when she asked me on an official date. By then, I already felt like I knew her, respected her, understood her in ways that I hadn't before. That was just before Christmas 2010.

This is Christmas 2011. A year of dating turned out to be a year of bliss, and now that I understood all of these various aspects of my lover, I had also come to understand how delightfully shy she really was.

Once she had identified herself as vanilla to me, it took her a long time to convince me she could be otherwise. It wasn't that I didn't believe her—I spotted the inner bottom in her a mile away—I just loved teasing her. I loved torturing her. I loved the way she'd blush and become tongue-tied whenever I asked about her fantasies. Pushed to talk about what she wanted, she'd admit that she wanted to be taken, that she fantasized about being dominated and that she really wanted me to have my way with her. This was all music to my ears, and I did have my way. A lot.

So when she asked for *an experience* and when I then came up with the idea of going to a cozy chocolatey retreat on an island, I also had something else in mind.

Only two days after I told her what the present was, we were off. We each carried a backpack. Hers had her clothes and a waterproof jacket so we could hike, even in the rain. Mine was mostly filled with sex toys. We got on the ferry and forgot all about our lives back home. Everything blurred as we crossed the channel in the typical misty rainy West Coast weather.

From the ferry terminal, we hiked along a winding path up the side of a mountain to the village where we met one of the chocolatiers. He showed us to our room, gave us the key and told us he'd bring us Americano coffees and biscotti in the morning.

"Perfect," I said, locking the door as soon as he left.

"It's gorgeous," my lover said, looking around. She started exploring the pamphlets left out on the dresser about the area, but I was more interested in exploring her.

"Let's check out the shower," I said.

"Mmm," she moaned. "Sounds fantastic."

We opened the door to the bathroom and immediately she commented on the craftsmanship of the shower tiles, how nicely they'd been laid. I appreciate a knowledgeable butch and her eye for detail. I unbuttoned the top button of her shirt and she did the rest. Our clothes were on the floor almost immediately and she adjusted the knobs in the shower to get the temperature just right.

Underneath the steamy steady flow of water, we held each other and exhaled.

"I don't know how my breasts got so dirty," I said. "You'd better lather them up. You wouldn't want to be stuck out here in the woods with a filthy girl, would you?"

"Maybe I would," she said, taking the orange-scented soap in her hands and lathering. Once she had a nice mass of bubbles, she took my breasts in her hands and smeared the frothy soap all over them. My nipples responded to her touch and I could feel my clit doing the same. After some delicious kissing in the wetness of the shower, I needed to get her on the bed.

We toweled off in the bathroom and she got dressed in her new pajamas, my stocking present to her. They fit perfectly and she looked adorable. Sometimes all I want is to cozy up to her and cuddle with her. I love the way our bodies feel next to each other and I love the way she looks in pajamas, but it wasn't what I wanted at that moment. I let her try out the bed while I stayed in the bathroom and changed into my new lingerie, a lacy lavender camisole that barely touched my thighs.

"Wow," she said when I came out, "you look beautiful."

"Really?" I smiled, ever so delighted.

"Yes," she said. "You're so pretty. You're so sexy. I'm so lucky."

"I'm the lucky one." I went into my backpack and pulled out a locked black box containing all of the goodies I'd brought. I carried it over to the side table and set it down. Her eyes widened. I clicked the box open and pulled out the restraints.

"Oooh," she gasped.

Then I pulled out the candles.

"Oh, my," she said.

Finally, I pulled out a bottle of massage oil.

"Take your shirt off," I said, "I want to rub you."

She took it off. I climbed on top of her, straddling her the way I do when I want to orgasm. She still had her pajama bottoms on. I gave her hips a squeeze with my inner thighs and then I rubbed my breasts in her face because I couldn't help myself. I can never help myself.

I held the bottle of oil up, and from several feet above her, I let a couple of drops fall. Then a couple more. I started to rub her chest with the oil and then leaned down and whispered in her ear.

"I have something special planned for you."

"I can't wait," she said.

"You'll have to," I replied. "It's for tomorrow."

"Oh?"

She gave me her best sad puppy eyes, so I told her that tonight was just a prelude. As I rubbed her shoulders and chest with oil, I told her what tomorrow would bring.

"I want to restrain you," I said, taking hold of her wrists with my hands. I leaned down on them. "I want to take away your ability to move."

"Mmm-hmm," she moaned.

"And then I want to slather you with oil," I continued as I went back to massaging her chest. I concentrated on her breasts, squeezing her nipples between my forefinger and thumb. "Then I want to take this candle…"

I reached into the box and pulled out the dark red beeswax candle. "And I want to drop melted wax on you."

She didn't say anything, but only because she was nervous. Her smile told me everything I needed to know.

"You see, this weekend, we're corrupting you. You may have been an innocent pornographer up until this point, but you're about to be hardcore."

"Oooh," she moaned. "I want you to pop my kink cherry."

"Oh, I know you do."

"I want you to do anything you want with me."

"Oh really," I said.

"Yes."

"You dirty slut," I said.

"Oh yeah." She nodded.

"You're not vanilla at all, are you?"

She shook her head.

"Yeah," I said, "I didn't think so."

I took off her pajama bottoms and pulled out the oil again. This time I held it up over her pussy and, like before, squeezed out a couple of drops.

"This is what it'll be like when I drop wax onto you," I explained, "only it'll be hot."

"This *is* hot."

"It sure is," I agreed. I massaged her pussy from her belly downward and from her inner thighs inward. Finally, I arrived at the wetness. I ran my fingers over her and gasped in delight.

"You are so kinky, my love. Just look at how wet you are thinking all your dirty, dirty thoughts about tomorrow."

"I know. I am."

"You're a pervert."

"I am! I am a pervert."

"And I'm so glad," I whispered. Then I reached behind her for a pillow and propped her hips on it. "I want to lick your pussy for a while before I let you strap on your cock and fuck me."

She nodded eagerly and moaned beneath my tongue. She let her hips relax into the moment, let me slide my tongue up and down her delectable opening. When we both became too eager, too aroused to stand it any longer, she reached for the vibrator. She buzzed herself into a blissful cloud of ecstasy. My own pussy, meanwhile, throbbed and ached in desperation.

She went to the bathroom and came back adorned by her sexy cock. When she lay back down, I straddled her again. I rode her cock up and down as she squeezed my nipples and watched me wriggle in delight. She grabbed onto my breasts and took my nipples in her mouth one at a time, alternating back and forth in precisely the way she knows that I love. I moaned and writhed and then bucked on top of her as a massive orgasm built within me and exploded all over her. Deflated, I sighed and exhaled and rested on her chest, her cock still inside me. My muscles pulsated around her and she held me tight as I experienced the overwhelming relief I needed.

When I finally flipped over on my back, she slipped out of her leather strap-on and sat up.

"Oh," she said, almost ladylike, "what's over here?"

She reached for the box of organic chocolates.

"Oh, yeah," I moaned. "Let's open it."

"It'll be like an after-sex cigarette, only way better," she joked. She has never been a smoker.

The box contained twelve filled truffle chocolates in various shapes and with various outer dips. We each selected one. She put hers in her mouth and began moaning again, this time even louder than when she climaxed.

"Oh my god," she said, "it's sea salt and caramel and dark chocolate ganache."

I took a bite of mine and immediately related to her sounds. I could feel them coming out of me as well.

"Oh my god," I exclaimed, "this one is kind of spicy and cinnamony with a creamy center."

The chocolate coated my tongue with a rich velvety layer of perfection. We discovered heaven. Over the course of the evening, we became so acquainted with heaven that all twelve divine morsels disappeared. We even invented a new term: *mouth-gasm*.

The following day, we woke up to Americanos and biscotti at our door. We kissed each other, sipped our espresso beverages and relived the memories of the night before. We made arrangements for another box of chocolates and then, like good lesbians, we went for a hike in the surrounding woods. For two hours, we clambered up and down the forest terrain, making our way around a beautiful lake. We talked about resolutions, feelings and everything that came to mind.

Part of what I treasure so much about my lover is that we can have the most amazing mind-blowing sex and we can also revert to our days of being walking buddies. We can talk about anything. Or nothing. Sometimes it's nice to just walk together in silence.

But once we neared our room, I confessed to her that I'd been thinking of nothing but this adventure ever since the first week of December and I couldn't wait to get her back to bed so I could play with her.

Back in our room, I showered first. Then I sent her in. While she was in the shower, I went into my backpack and pulled out a sheet I'd brought from home. The main hazard of wax play (that is, if proper safety procedures are followed) is ruined sheets. I also affixed the wrist restraints to the bed. I put the candles on the table, got a lighter out and clicked open the bottle of massage oil.

I folded up my lover's pajamas and put them on her side table. She came out of the bathroom with a chocolate-brown towel wrapped around her. She saw the arranged bed and immediately her shyness came out. Instinctively, she went for her pajamas.

"Not so fast," I said. "You won't be needing them."

She gulped. "Somehow I thought you might say that."

"I have something else for you to do instead."

"What's that?"

"Come here."

She came over. I sat her down on the bed.

"Your task is to sit here," I said, patting the middle of the bed where I'd propped up some pillows. "I want you to come here and find a position you'll be comfortable in."

She complied, but I could tell she was nervous, so I kissed her, long and slow, and as our tongues found each other, I could feel her tension disappear.

"I'm not going to do anything you won't like," I said. But then I thought about it for a moment and added, "At least, if I do, it'll be an accident and I'll stop immediately if you say you don't like it."

"I trust you," she said.

"Good," I said, "I never want to do anything to jeopardize that. I love you."

"I love you, too."

"Now come here and give me your wrists."

"Okay." She smiled.

"You're so willing to do whatever I say," I observed. "No resistance whatsoever. You must be more of a pervert than I thought, my little bottom."

She giggled. "I am."

In seconds, her wrists were behind her head, interlocked with each other and attached to the frame of the solid wood bed.

"How's that?" I asked.

"It feels great."

"Try to get loose."

She wriggled and struggled.

"It's no fun if you're not truly rendered helpless."

"I can't move," she said.

"Oh good."

I straddled her, like I'd done the day before. This time, our pussies touched and I was well aware that she could feel just how wet I was.

I held the oil above her and teased her a little with it before I squirted some out. It splashed down on her naked, helpless chest and began to dribble down her. I squeezed the bottle some more and watched carefully as the drops fell. Then I slathered the oil all over her, taking special care to squeeze her nipples each time I passed over them.

I excused myself, went to the bathroom and came back with scissors.

"What do you think these are for?" I asked. "Nervous?"

She shook her head. "Maybe a little."

Then I held up the hand-dipped beeswax candles and snipped

the wick between them. I put the scissors down along with one
of the candles. She looked relieved.

I caressed her with the candle, passing it over her chest like it
was a wand that would create a new kind of magic for her.

Then I lit the candle and held it upright for a while to let her
get used to the idea.

"Does this make you nervous?" I asked.

"I used to be a firefighter, remember?" she replied. "I used to
have to run into burning buildings."

"Yes, but you weren't tied up and helpless, were you?"

"No."

"And you weren't being straddled by a kinky pervert who
enjoys inflicting pain."

"Unfortunately, I was not."

I nodded. Then I whispered, "Good answer."

Holding the candle with my right hand, I put my left palm
over her chest. "I think you're ready."

I moved my left hand.

Ever so slowly, I tilted the candle. It dripped. Smack. A drop
of hot wax hit her chest and she gasped. It hardened immediately. So did her nipples. I moved my hand a little and another
drop of wax fell on her. She flinched.

"It hurts more than I thought it would," she said.

"Too much?"

"No. I like it."

"I thought you might."

We found a beautiful rhythm. My dripping, her wincing and
flinching and squirming and resisting her natural desire to resist.
Moment by moment, we were intensely present, hyperaware of
any and all changes.

I let the wax drip over her, inching closer and closer to her
left nipple and finally right on it. She held her breath. When I

thought she'd had enough, I let her have one more drop and then I stopped. I blew out the candle and put it down.

"That was really intense," she said.

"That was just half the fun. It's also fun when it comes off."

I got a plastic card out and began to scrape the wax off, drop by drop. She moaned.

"That feels good," she said.

I nodded.

I held her and told her I was proud of her, that she was a great bottom and that I loved her.

"And now I'm going to lick your pussy and I want you to direct me because, you see, I want to make you come that way."

"I don't want to direct you."

"Too bad. You have to."

"Um, okay." She gulped. "I guess it's all about endurance. Oh, and up-and-down motion, but not too heavy."

"Oh, now see? There you go. That's good direction."

My tongue made its way to her wetness and I did just as she said, feeling so privileged to be there with her, honored that she was letting me have my way with her. I really wanted nothing more than to let her body release all of the tension that I could feel she had built up. All of that anticipation. All of those heightened nerves. The intensity of surrendering to someone else's whims and giving up control so that I could take it. I appreciated her so much in that moment. Up and down, my tongue explored the landscape of her labia, made its way over the summit of her clit. Up and down. I could have kept going forever and ever. This was better than chocolate, even organic hand-crafted chocolate. And then she began to writhe and pulsate and moan. I kept my movements as steady as I could. She gasped.

"Oh my god. Oh my god," I heard her say.

Moments later, having released her from her restraints, I held her in my arms.

"You're a bona fide kinky pervert," I said. "You can hold your head up high at any play party from now on, my sweet sexy bottom."

She smiled. I cradled her in my arms.

"And now for a mouth-gasm," I said, reaching for the box of chocolates. She chose one of the filled chocolates and took a bite. Then she moaned and I watched the tip of her tongue slowly disappear into the creamy center of the truffle.

"Oh my god. Oh my god!" she cried out.

A look of peaceful ecstasy came over her as she savored every sweet moment of the chocolate. I stroked her skin while her body returned to its characteristically calm equilibrium. I held her close, absorbing the bliss of our connection.

Then I had my way with her again. And again.

FOXY AND THE RIDICULOUS LESBIAN ORGY

Allison Moon

Whoever finds the fox, gets to fuck the fox. These are the words written on the dry erase board of my living room. There are twenty-five half-naked women in my apartment, it is almost two a.m., and the fox hunt is about to begin.

But I'm getting ahead of myself.

When a friend needed an extra "girl on girl" story for her live storytelling event, I volunteered immediately. I'd been fucking girls long enough, so I knew there had to be a story in my past somewhere. But a week later, I was racking my brain for a good story and coming up empty. Well, there was that time when we ran into Baptists while skinny-dipping, but it wasn't very sexy. Then there was that epic Scrabble game, but no. I did remember a great story involving my ex and a gnarly yeast infection, but if I told that story onstage I would never get laid again.

I think the problem I was having is that cock is always funny, all the time, but I take pussy very, very seriously.

I had no story to tell, but the flyers had gone out, and time was short. I had no choice. For the sake of science—nay, for the sake of art, I had to take matters into my own hands. I had to throw a Ridiculous Lesbian Orgy.

Now, I know what you're thinking. If you construct the context for a story, are you actually experiencing the story, or just experiencing yourself experiencing the story, thus negating the veracity of the experience? If it's really happening but in an artificial context, does it count as "true"? I'm a writer, these are the things I think about. Nevertheless, I figured if the story had enough hot dyke action, no one would really care if I pulled a bit of a James Frey up on stage.

I've never read *The Secret*, but living in NorCal, you tend to absorb it from your surroundings. I think the gist is that you send a powerful request out into the universe, and the universe reciprocates.

Well, I emailed out the invitation to the Ridiculous Lesbian Orgy and not three minutes later I hear from downstairs, "Hey, Allie?"

It's my roommate, Lydia. "Hey, Allie? My mom's visiting this weekend. It's cool that she stays here, right?"

My brain screams, "NO! No, it's not okay! I'm throwing a Ridiculous Lesbian Orgy! Your mom can't be here!"

But then I hear a mild, new-agey voice in my head saying, "Allison, you called this into being. You can't just send it away."

So instead, I say, "Sure, Lydia, that's okay. No, in fact, I *insist* your mother stay here this weekend."

I sent out the invitation on a Tuesday. On Friday night, my apartment is filled with twenty-five half-naked women, and already I consider this a success.

The ridiculous starts right away. We have Hitachi races, if you know what I mean. And we have Hitachi Jeopardy, which is very, very difficult. Try conjugating French verbs next time you're having an orgasm. Seriously, just try it.

If you've been to an orgy or play party before, you know that there tend to be waves of excitement. There's the first fuck-hungry hump fest that happens early in the evening when everyone's nervous and excited. Then it kind of mellows out and everyone ends up snarfing at the snack table or processing in the bathtub for a while. The next wave happens rather late, when everyone is finally asking for what they *really* want and fucking who they *really* want to. Freshly bathed and full of hummus, we're approaching the second wave when my friend decides that she wants a scene of a fox hunt. It's the night before the royal wedding and everyone's feeling kind of sentimental about Britain, so we say sure, we'll do that.

Foxy congregates seven women and starts explaining the details of a traditional fox hunt in her beautiful (real) British accent. The rest of us look warily to one another saying, "None of us signed up for blood-play."

Foxy assures us that there will be no cutting off of tails and stamping foreheads with bloody stumps. Instead, we'll rip off the bandana she has stuck in the waistband of her underwear, and then we'll fuck her.

And we look to one another and say, "Oh we can totally do that. Yes, we're in. Let's go."

She goes on to say we'll each have a role. There's going to be a hunt mistress and hunters and hound dogs and horses. As she's explaining this, my friend Glo shouts "Wait!" and runs over to her bag and pulls out...a bunch of animal hats. There's a bunny rabbit, a panda bear, a tiger, amazingly enough a fox and there's... a wolf. Now, you should know I have a penchant for wolves, specifically lesbian werewolves, since I spent the past three years of my life writing and publishing a novel about them.

I put on the wolf hat and it seals the deal. I'm in it, finding my inner furry and deciding that she's a pretty rad little wolf. I start to growl and bare my teeth. My fingers curl like paws and I pull against Tiger's arm as she holds me in place like the good hunter she is. Foxy has us put on strap-ons, so we harness up while we whip ourselves into a frenzy, stretching and jumping, barking and cheering. At this point we're all a little fuck drunk and drunk drunk, so we start going there...fast.

We're blaring trumpets, I'm barking like a big ol' hound dog, we're shouting and making a hell of a ruckus, when we hear a key in the front door.

We are seven women standing in my living room, in bras, panties, huge hard-ons and animal hats.

And my roommate walks in with her mother.

We stop. We plaster on sweet smiles and call out "Hi!!!" like we're preteens at a slumber party.

Lydia's mom pauses in the living room, takes in the scene and waves. We wave back. She says, "Okay! Nice to meet you," and hurries into the guest room and shuts the door behind her.

We launch right back into the trumpet blares and woofing.

We sound the trumpet. Foxy gets a thirty-second head start and tears off up the stairs. We hear her heavy footsteps overhead as she tries to find a hiding spot. The footsteps clatter for a bit and then silence.

A thing you should know about my apartment is that it's a rather big loft, but it's not, say, *English countryside* big. So Foxy gets her head start, but there's not a lot of places to hide.

We charge up the stairs en masse, letting the hunt mistress, Bunny Rabbit, lead the way. She runs to the sitting room and sniffs and waits. Nothing.

Then she leads us to my office. We wait. Nothing.

Then she creeps to the door of my bedroom. We listen, my

wolf ears rotating like little satellite dishes. There's an intense pause. Then with a clatter and an explosion of dirty underwear, Foxy bursts from my hamper. She leaps to my bed to try to escape, but I'm right there and let my newly acquired animal instincts lead the way.

I grab her around the waist and drag her to the floor. She's on top of me kicking and screaming and biting and punching, but I'm holding tight. The girls are screeching "Flip her over! Flip her over! Flip her over!"

Foxy elbows me in the chest as I flip her over, and I get her ass in the air and her face is buried in my tits. Bunny Rabbit rushes over, grabs the bandana from the back of her underwear, holds it triumphantly above her head, then throws it to the ground. Foxy fights, but she knows she's done for. Bunny Rabbit takes a condom from the top of my bureau and slowly rolls it on her cock.

There's a moment of reverent silence as we all realize, *Oh my. This is a gang bang.*

Bunny Rabbit yanks Foxy's underwear down to her knees while I've still got her pinned. She struggles against me, but she's surrendering. Her face is buried so deep in my tits that all I can see of her face is that fox hat. It's staring up at me with these sweet, brown mendicant eyes. I think, *Oh, poor Foxy, you should've run faster.*

Bunny Rabbit lives up to her namesake and gives it to Foxy really good, her ears flopping over her face as she humps like, well, a rabbit. Then Tiger is up with her hot pink harness and dildo, and Foxy groans into my rib cage. Despite the carpet burn I acquired in wrestling Foxy to the ground, I enjoy the massage on my back as we rock back and forth on a pile of my dirty drawers. By now she's given up fighting completely and is just holding on tight as the women take her in turns.

A procession of be-dildoed women take on the fox, punishing her for her impertinent running and hiding. In the meantime, the rest of the partygoers have crept upstairs, sitting on chairs and pillows in a semicircle around my bedroom's open door. One of them is passing around snacks.

Finally, it's Panda Bear's turn. She's excited and insists we all call her Mei Sheng. The harness hits her in the right spots and she's moaning more than Foxy is. From my vantage, all I can see is Foxy's little fox face staring up at me. Then cresting over her shoulder there's a little plush panda face staring at me with vacant black eyes. I wonder, is this where Red Pandas come from?

Foxy's near her limit but it's still my turn. I edge out from beneath her and roll a condom onto my fingers to give her a break from all the cock. I ease my fingers into her. She's wet and gaping. As I milk her G-spot whilst all my friends watch through the bedroom's open door, and the moans and shouts of other women echo throughout my loft, I have one singular thought: The Secret fucking works.

Talk about declaring something powerfully. The Secret is the reason I had twenty-five naked dykes humping in my apartment. It's is the reason I discovered my inner furry, okay? I'm proud of that. The Secret is the reason my besties and I strapped on animal hats and cocks and whaled on our buddy until she couldn't take any more. The Secret is the reason I was able to get hella laid after I told the story onstage. And you know what else? I think the Secret can save the world. Seriously. Because I've never met anyone else who could convince a panda to mate in captivity.

NURSE JOAN

Cheyenne Blue

At night, the O.R. is a place of dark, mysterious corners. The operating table is a gleam of dull chrome in the subdued light, and there's an anticipatory breathlessness to the place. In the wee small hours, you'd swear that the ghosts reclaim their territory.

I flitted silently through the operating suite, checking stock levels before the day shift arrived. Swabs, syringes, sutures. This was my time of the night, the time when I was most alert, and I loved being awake and alone in the O.R. As the most junior nurse, still in my final student year, the others were happy to leave me the drudgework.

She came up behind me when I least expected it. Only the suggestion of breath in the air told me I was no longer alone. Then her hand rested lightly on my shoulder, finding the skin at the neck of my scrubs.

"Stocking up?" Joan asked, although she could see the answer from the stack of sterile drapes on my trolley.

I nodded silently.

"Good girl." There was amusement in her rich voice. Her hand drifted down my arm to take the drape from my fingers.

I fought to suppress a shiver. I'd had a crush on Joan ever since I started night duty. She was West Indian and had come to London years before to do her nursing training. With her wide flat hips, dark-chocolate skin and expressive eyes—rich and ripe like purple sloes—she was my ideal woman. And her swaying gait as she ambled the corridors between the operating rooms made me long to put my hand on her ass to feel how she undulated underneath my touch.

I knew she had a girlfriend—the good-natured teasing of the other nurses had imparted that information. So even if I'd had the courage, I didn't think she was within the realm of possibility.

Joan placed the drape on the shelf and leaned against the cabinet with folded arms. "Why do you have the lights so low? Why don't you turn them up?"

I shrugged. "It's more peaceful this way. I can see enough."

Her gaze ran deliberately over my body. "So can I."

My breath hitched in my throat. Her unexpected flirting chased thrills of heat over my skin.

"You got much more to do?" She gestured to the trolley.

"No. This is the last load."

"Maybe there's time for some in-service training, then." Her bold stare caught me full in the face, her mouth lifting in a crook-corner smile.

I swallowed hard, my heart pounding. I was positive she didn't simply mean a lecture on anesthetic drugs—but what did she have in mind?

She moved further out into the shadowy room. "The bloody technician hasn't put away the table equipment again." Her hand waved over the jumble of armrests, brackets and poles piled haphazardly on a shelf in the corner. "Why don't we go over patient positioning and safety?"

"If you want," I replied.

Joan folded her arms. "Tell me how you'd position a patient for a left nephrectomy."

"Well," I started, "right lateral position. Lower arm bent, slightly out from the body. Upper arm on a padded arm support. To maximize the angle between the ribs and pelvis, the table..."

"Show me how you'd attach the supports."

I picked up a clamp and support. "The forearm must be supported without any pressure—" I broke off. "It's easier to show than tell."

Joan smiled slightly. "So I'll be the patient." Leaving her clogs on the floor, she hopped onto the table and lay on her back, arms by her sides.

"It will be easier if you turn on your side."

"What's wrong, Gill? Worried you can't turn me? C'mon. Any O.R. nurse has to be able to turn patients alone. What if I vomited? Would you dither while I aspirated?"

"Of course not." But doing it alone meant bending down so that my breasts brushed her side. It meant sliding my hand between her thighs, grasping the lower and flipping her in one deft movement. I'd done it thousands of times, and you get immune to patients' bodies when you're a nurse. You don't think about their breasts, their bellies, the curve of their ass, the plumpness of their thighs. This shouldn't be any different. But it was.

I tried not to think about my hand between her legs; dangerous thoughts, laden with implications. In one movement I flipped her so that she lay on her side, limp, her limbs heavy as I went about methodically pushing padding between her thighs, ensuring that the upper arm was well supported with no pull on the shoulder. Her body was solid underneath the thin scrubs, and much as I wanted to, I didn't linger on the exposed skin of her arms. Finally, I cranked the table so that she was stretched over in an arc, and tilted her chin with a finger so that her airway was clear. Her scrubs parted at the waist, showing a wedge of smooth skin.

"There," I said. "That should do it."

"You should have ensured my airway was clear first," she grumbled. "Now show me where the incision would be."

Lightly, I traced a line over the exposed skin at her waist.

She shivered underneath my fingers, but her voice was steady. "Well done. Now let me out of here, and we'll try another position."

Her shiver made me bold. I unstrapped her from the table. "You show me how it's done."

Joan didn't miss a beat as she swung her feet to the floor. "Fine. Anterior resection. Lie on the table." Her eyes held a hint of a challenge, and I knew why. That surgical position involved raising the patient's legs and spreading them in padded poles so that the surgeon could sit between.

She saw, and one eyebrow arched. "Afraid your trousers will split?"

Scrubs were as loose as they were practical. "Hardly."

I climbed onto the narrow table and lay on my back as Joan had done. Firmly she secured my arms so they couldn't drop. Her strong fingers whispered over my ribs. As she leaned over to check the far side, her breasts lightly brushed mine. The shock was abrupt and perfect. I forced myself to lie still, breathing in even rhythm as her hands patted over my sides, ostensibly checking that my arms were correctly positioned.

Then she moved to the foot of the table and clamped the bulky leg stirrups into place.

"Ideally, there should be two people positioning the legs," she lectured. "Why is that so?"

"The legs have to be lifted together to avoid putting strain on the lower back," I chanted in reply.

"Well, there's only me here, so shuffle down, please."

"I can't," I complained. "You've secured my arms."

A deep sigh, then Joan tugged at the canvas underneath me. I lifted my legs for her and she positioned one in each stirrup. She removed the end section of the table and, standing between my legs, dragged the canvas until my butt rested on the very edge of the table. Moving swiftly, she made final adjustments to the angles of the stirrups, swinging them out so that my hips screamed in protest.

Lightly she touched the angle of thigh and groin. "Your hips are tight. If you were under anesthetic, you'd be more relaxed."

"But I'm not," I grumbled. "It hurts."

Her hand came down on my belly, moving in slow circles. Not quite a massage, nearly a caress. "Relax. You're too tight here." Her hand moved to my groin and her fingers dug deeply into the crease. "Obviously you don't spread your legs often enough."

The pressure from her fingers was fierce, but not painful enough to stop me reacting to her closeness. Her belly brushed my hip, and her free hand rested familiarly on my shoulder.

Nurses are tactile people; we're always touching: holding patients' hands, dealing with their intimate body functions, staring at their unclothed bodies with our professional eyes. And we touch each other with friendly familiarity. It's as if our body zones expand to include each other. But this night, Joan's touch went beyond that.

I stared up at the ceiling, where the recessed lighting shone as dim points in the clinical roof. Joan touched my shoulder. "Tell me how else I could secure a patient's arms."

"Using their gown," I replied.

Joan unfastened my arms and folded them high over my chest. Tugging at the loose scrubs top, she succeeded in working it up, enough that my belly was bared to the cool air. A particularly hard tug and I heard the thin cotton tear at the back.

"Whoops," she said, no trace of remorse in her voice. "But that makes it easier."

In an instant, my arms were tightly bound to my body with my cotton top. The cool air lapped at my skin. I shivered, not only from the temperature, but also from the knowledge that Joan was staring down at me, at the underside of my breasts, at my exposed abdomen. I struggled slightly, the vulnerability of the position making me uncomfortable.

"You'd better release me now," I said. "Before…"

"Before what?" Joan's lilting voice replied. "Before someone comes? Before you come? You've wanted to get like this with me for weeks now, girlie. Why d'you now want out?"

I flushed, mortified she'd read me so easily, and tried to free my arms. But she'd done too good a job: my arms were bound tightly to my body and my legs were strapped to the heavy poles. No, I was stuck here until she deigned to let me go.

Her fingers traced light circles on my belly, around and around my navel, ever-widening, concentric spirals of pleasure. I struggled in a futile attempt to escape the stirrups and wondered why I was even trying. Didn't she have me exactly where I wanted to be?

"You can't get away until I let you," she said as her fingers inched underneath the waistband of my pants. "Do you want me to stop, Gill?"

Her fingers imprinted themselves on my skin, her pinkie lightly flicking the elastic of my panties.

"Well?" she demanded, when I didn't answer. "Do you want me to stop?" She withdrew an infinitesimal amount, and it was enough to loosen my vocal cords.

"No," I croaked.

"No what?"

"Please don't stop, Joan."

And she returned, tracing along the elastic with infinite slowness, a crawling light touch that ignited a fire down deep in my belly. I'd always lusted after her, a sort of longing hope-lessness. Now, it seemed, it was mutual. When her fingers slid down to cup my mound, the abruptness of it would have jolted my legs out of the stirrups if they hadn't been strapped down. Her fingers drummed a light pattern before edging underneath the elastic. She tugged lightly on my hairs.

Her eyes were half-closed, and a small smile tilted her lips upward. She was intent on discovery, and now that our lust was fully out in the open she was bold. Her fingers journeyed down, then reversed direction to tease my lips, the gentlest of touches, in complete contrast to her manner of a moment ago. I longed to reach down and press her hand more firmly against myself, direct her touch, show her how I liked it, but of course, I couldn't.

She must have read my mind, seen my longing, but she only shifted closer, so that her belly brushed against my bound arm. Her fingers drummed a light pattern on my clit. "You like this, white girl?"

"Yes." The word half-choked as Joan circled my clit with a warm finger.

"What would you like me to do?"

A dozen scenarios flashed through my head: Joan tearing

away my trousers to fuck me with a thick fist, Joan sitting between my straining thighs using her fingers and tongue to bring me to a shuddering climax, Joan getting creative with surgical clamps on my nipples and labia. I wanted them all, but there was one thing I wanted more.

"Let my arms free so I can touch you."

"Nice thought. That can come later. But first..." She paused in thought, and her skilful fingers paused too. "I think you're wearing too many clothes." She slowly withdrew her hand, moved around to stand between my strapped legs and picked a pair of surgeon's scissors from the trolley. The metal was cold against my calf as she slid the blades along my leg, cutting open the cotton scrubs from ankle to groin. They fell away and she continued around in a long arc, back down the other leg. A swift flash of metal and my panties were gone. Joan tugged the ruined material from underneath me.

And then she was back, pulling up a stool, sitting down so that her face was level with my cunt and so close that I could feel her puffs of breath.

Our first kiss was the most intimate kiss of all: her face between my legs, her lips and tongue working over my sex. She teased, she probed, she lapped, and all the while the fire in my belly burned hotter, the spiral of need wound tighter. My hands clenched into fists within the confining material, and I closed my eyes and let the sensations build. My world narrowed down to touch: the ache of my hips strained wide on the poles, the constriction of my arms against my chest, the coolness of the air on my exposed belly, and most of all, Joan's tongue rasping over my pussy lips, dancing with pinpoint accuracy on my clit. When she added her fingers to the mix, pistoning in and out of my cunt, the tension exploded in one long spasm. I came hard, clamping around her fingers, pushing my cunt hard against her mouth. The release was so fierce it was almost painful.

I sighed, feeling my muscles relax, and instantly the tension on my hips eased. Moisture trickled down my pussy, down to the crack of my ass, although whether it was my fluids or her saliva I didn't know. I opened my eyes to the sight of the dim ceiling with the operating light hovering over me like an other-worldly starship.

Joan stood and came back to the head of the table. Her fingers brushed my lips, leaving a salty taste. They smelled like me.

"So, white girl," she said softly, "do you think you'll remember how to position a patient for anterior resection now?" Her hands were busy, releasing my arms.

When one hand was free, I snaked it out and grasped her by the back of the neck, pulling her down to me for a soft kiss. She tasted of smoke and vanilla, a heady mix.

"Maybe I need more practice," I said. "Tomorrow night, I'll put you in the same position, and you can check if I get it right."

RING OF ROSES

Giselle Renarde

I spent three hours crying in her bed.

She was right there, snoring beside me, yet I couldn't get past the gnawing sensation that she'd never be mine, not entirely. Her house was full of meaningful knickknacks and mementoes, little reminders of a marriage that, in my mind, would never cease to exist. Was there really room for me?

There were photographs everywhere, in every room. Why so goddamn many photographs? Why did I have to look at them? Or better yet, why couldn't I see past them? *I'm the girl who's sleeping in her bed, the girl she chats with every night, the girl she pulls into the shower with her, and that's all that matters.* I tried to comfort myself with those thoughts, but I guess I savored my sadness too much. There were certain things neither of us would release—Danielle had her pictures, I had my pain.

Danielle had told me many times that I was being juvenile, and I knew she was right, but I could never reconcile my emotions. "I don't know why you let things get to you," she often said. "Let my actions speak for me."

But I only saw her inactions. I only saw the photographs still hanging on the wall.

That's why I booked the couples package in Niagara Falls, complete with king-sized bed, in-room Jacuzzi tub, and a dozen red roses. We still had a few more days we'd committed to spending together, and I just couldn't stand another night in her bed, haunted by those all-too-real pictures of a ghost marriage. Instead, I would whisk my girl off on a surprise getaway for two. Perfect.

I guess I could have told this story as a sickly sweet romance with me as the gallant sugar mama. It still would have been objectively true, but it wouldn't have been the complete and unadulterated truth. If I'm going for honesty, I might as well go all the way, even if the reality makes me seem immature and a little bit crazy.

You should have seen her face when I announced the trip. I'd never seen her so ecstatic. She rushed to fetch her suitcase and I sat on the bed while she riffled through her closet, holding outfits up against her body. "I wonder if this still fits... Oooh, a cleavage dress!"

For the first time since I'd arrived at this house I was never comfortable in, I felt happy and hopeful. Danielle's joy gave me that gift.

"Where are you taking me for dinner?" she asked.

"The Brazilian steakhouse."

Her eyes lit up. "That place is expensive!"

Everything was expensive, but there was only one perfect response to that statement: "Anything for my girl."

We arrived in Niagara just after noon and took a walk by the falls. The weather was mild for January in Canada, cottonball snowflakes melting as they hit the pavement. When the breeze turned cool, I led my girlfriend the amateur photographer to the horticultural center so she could practice her hobby on bright tropical plants.

This whole trip might have been spur of the moment, but I knew Danielle well enough to plot adventures she would appreciate. Her happiness was truly my greatest joy, though she'd probably tell you my greatest joy was getting laid. Maybe we were both right.

When we went back to the hotel to dress for dinner, Danielle admired the blood-red roses I'd organized for the room. I wanted to be the only person in the world who'd ever bought her roses, and it was a strange source of anguish that I couldn't change the past to make that true. I wanted to. I wanted to wipe out her history, but all I could do was give her roses and steak dinners and jewelry and hotel stays, and hope to one day supersede everything that came before me.

If I hadn't already.

I threw on the best outfit I'd brought and then sat on the ledge of the Jacuzzi tub, watching my girlfriend meticulously applying her makeup. Every time, I felt like a kid again. It was like watching my mother get ready for her office Christmas parties back in the day. The dusty rose scent of loose powder brought back a lost sort of magic.

Danielle put on a necklace I hadn't bought her, and I hated how much that irked me. Wasn't it enough that she was wearing not one but two rings I'd given her? Did I need to dress her like a child, pick out jewels from among those I'd purchased? Hell, maybe I could just own her outright and keep her in a cage. Then I'd never have to feel jealous.

The woman I loved had a past. I needed to accept that, or we'd fall apart. I could feel us tearing at the seams already.

"Well?" she asked, doing a little turn. "How do I look?"

I'd told her a hundred times she was the most beautiful woman I'd ever met, but she never took my compliments to heart. In that low-cut black dress, she took my breath away. I didn't even get a chance to plant my face between her boobs before she was reaching around me for her coat, saying, "Come on! We're already late for dinner."

Dinner! Now that she was dressed to the nines, all I wanted to eat was her.

But Brazilian steak was a close second. The meal was delicious and the setting romantic beyond belief. Our conversations had that giddy early-relationship feel, where you're fascinated by everything your date has to say. I couldn't stop smiling, and she rolled her eyes and grinned every time my gaze dipped down into her cleavage.

After dinner, we took a leisurely walk through the nearby casino and then headed out into the night, gripping each other tightly as we descended the slippery slope toward the falls. We arrived fallside just in time for the nine o'clock fireworks—a happy accident, which Danielle caught on film while I snuggled up against her.

Everything was perfect. Everything. I kept waiting for something to go wrong and then telling myself to keep the negativity at bay. *Just let this weekend be wonderful. Enjoy Danielle's company. Don't ruin it.*

After we'd walked back to the hotel and let our toes defrost, Danielle took off her makeup while I filled the large Jacuzzi tub. When the water level looked about right, I broke apart two long-stemmed roses and scattered the petals across our king-sized bed and over the gently steaming surface of our bath.

It was, by far, the most conventionally romantic thing I'd ever done, and even though Danielle and I always claimed to spurn convention, I think we both enjoyed the ambience those blood-red petals added to our room.

"Too bad we didn't bring any candles," I said as I stepped into the tub. "Would have been romantic."

I laughed when Danielle asked, "Should I join you?"

"I hope so!" I replied with a smile. "I didn't book a Jacuzzi suite so I could sit in here alone while you watch Letterman."

She stepped in, grinning. The tub was perfect for two, with enough space not to feel cramped and yet not so much that we were distanced from each other. My legs pressed against her side, and hers against mine. Red rose petals swirled around our bodies in figure eights while we gazed at each other, waiting for something to happen, wondering who should make the first move and what that move should be.

"Should we turn on the jets?" I asked, though the question sounded stupid even to my ears.

"Sure," Danielle said, like she was just happy to be along for the ride.

I pressed the button and the jets came to life, blasting me from every direction. The rose petals danced along the water's surface, some diving and bobbing, others finding my skin and latching on. I took one of the satiny petals and traced it along my sweetheart's jawline, then down her neck and across her shoulder.

"You have the smoothest skin I've ever touched." I felt it under the water, playing with her toes and making her squeal, padding my fingers up her calves as she inhaled deeply. "I love your legs, especially in heels."

"Especially in black thigh-highs." She'd worn them that evening, all black lingerie because she knew what I liked.

"Crap!" I said, squeezing her thigh. "We didn't take any pictures of us together, dressed for dinner."

"Oh well," she said simply. "Next time."

Would you believe I was still thinking about her walls back home? I wanted to see myself inside those frames—wanted to see *us* there. Was I crazy? I had to be, if I was going to let something so stupid ruin what had so far been the most beautiful day of our life together.

So I dove at my girlfriend's naked body, taking her freshly washed face in my hands and kissing her mouth. She never believed me when I said her perfect cherubic lips looked better without lipstick than with, but it was true. They were eternally plump, rosy red, gorgeous, and when they opened for my tongue I was ruthless.

The evening's pulpy romance came to a head in that moment, and she hugged me hard, returning my kisses as I pressed my naked body against hers. There was nothing better than feeling warm and wet all over while velvety petals hopped and danced against our skin. And though we were hardly afraid of the light, we usually made love in relative darkness. It was refreshing to get a good look at my girl's ample curves—the ones she referred to as "fat."

She touched my skin, brushing one hand down my ass while we consumed each other with kisses. Everything that led up to this moment kept playing though my mind: walking in the snow, pictures in the greenhouse, the sheer romance of dinner for two, and then fireworks over the falls. This was the absolute perfect ending to an absolutely perfect day.

I didn't notice at first that Danielle was sliding against the side of the tub. It didn't occur to me that we were sinking until my nose met the water. Danielle's face was completely submerged, and a panic struck me through as I struggled to right myself. We scrambled against the sides of the tub, laughing, no worse for the near drowning and, best of all, covered in rose petals.

"Are you trying to kill me?" she asked, giggling as she wiped water from her eyes.

"Why would I?" I teased. "It's not like I'd get anything out of it. I'm not even named in your will."

I shouldn't have made that joke. It made me think about things I preferred to ignore—like the legal rights we lacked because we weren't married, we didn't live together. *The photographs.* Every damn thing led back to them.

No sense in being sad on vacation. I put on a smile and turned in the tub, tossing my feet across the ledge. "I'm just going to get myself off on this jet. You can do whatever you want over there."

More teasing, and she knew it.

"Okay, fine," she said melodramatically. "Just ignore your girlfriend. You don't care about me anyway."

"Ha!" Sometimes I thought I cared too much about her, like she was my addiction. Anyway, Danielle was a total voyeur when it came to my pleasure. She loved watching me get off on my hand or my toys, or whatever did the trick—and this tub surely qualified!

Jacuzzi jets were new to us, but I knew how much she would love watching that blasting stream of water gush against my pussy. Grabbing hold of the little nozzle, I jerked it around and arched, gasping, when the jet struck my clit.

Right away, I turned to Danielle and saw my amazement reflected in the expression on her face. "Wow," she said with a visible shudder of excitement. "That looks good."

I loved her ability to sense my arousal vicariously, to actually feel my pleasure in her body. She was like some sort of sexual psychic.

"It feels amazing!" I closed my thighs for a moment and reached for one of the jet nozzles close to her, adjusting it to blast between her legs, though I could tell she was too far away to feel it. "You should try."

"I'm happier watching you," she said, which wasn't unusual. Sometimes Danielle wasn't keen on direct stimulation, whether it was my touch or a jet spray, but we'd been together long enough that I didn't take her occasional stoniness personally. After all, I enjoyed sensation enough for the both of us.

My breasts bobbed just above the water's burbling surface, my nipples hard as little pink pebbles. Rose petals kissed my bare skin like scarlet lips, and I took hold of one, smoothing it down my sweetheart's neck and chest, pressing it flush to one dark nipple and then the other.

Danielle's breath grew shallow—I could feel its pace quicken with each rise and fall of her chest—and when I looked into her eyes, I met the familiar darkness of her lust for me. For a moment, I thought she might plunge her head below the surface and eat my pussy underwater. Nothing turned me on better than watching her lick it.

"Open your legs," she said, reaching for my thigh. "Let me play with your pussy."

I smirked, adjusting my position, wanting the jet to find my clit again. "You just love my pussy, don't you?"

"Mmm-hmm!" she replied.

"You even love it when I say the word *pussy*."

Her eyes gleamed with knowing desire as she spread my lips with her fingers. I'd shaved for her, and being bare made my pussy even more sensitive than usual.

I gasped when the jet found my clit. "Oh my god, Danielle."

"That's good, huh?" That sneaky grin of hers turned me on every bit as much as her naked body, surrounded as it was by a bustling ring of rose petals. I reached between her thighs, stroking there, and she said, "What if I do this?"

Holding my bare pussy lips open with her index and ring fingers, she pressed on my clit with her middle finger and rubbed me off while the jet pummelled my pussy. Her insistent touch felt so good that I bucked up. Even when I arched my pelvis high out of the water, she didn't stop stroking me. God, she was good with her hands.

My clit was already so aching and engorged from the jet that Danielle's push launched me over the edge. It never took her long to make me come, but paired with a Jacuzzi jet, she got me off at record speed. Everything she did, whether it involved her fingers or her tongue or a vibrator or a cucumber, got me so worked up that I couldn't contain myself. I always said it was my attraction to her that lit the fire, and her touch that made me burn.

Danielle pushed my body back underwater, aligning my clit with the Jacuzzi jet. Once she had me where she wanted me, she grabbed the nozzle itself, turning it so it struck my throbbing clit in tight circles.

"Oh my god, baby!" I fucked the stream of water, splashing carelessly, and she grabbed my breast to settle me down. But once I got going, nothing could keep me from seeking out the next orgasm, and I begged her to pinch my nipple.

"Like this?" she teased, squeezing my tit between her thumb and forefinger.

"Yes!" I cried as a lightning bolt shot from my nipple straight down to my clit. "Do the other one."

"Like this?" she asked again, pressing on my other tit and then twisting it so hard it hurt.

"Yes, yes, yes!" I thrust my full weight against the Jacuzzi jet's stalwart blast, bringing a wave of water and rose petals with me. The wave crashed against the side of the tub and I let it carry me back, astounded by how light I felt in the hands of this warm bath.

In the midst of so much pleasure, I hadn't paid much attention to my girl's sweet body. I pressed my hand between her thighs, stroking while she pinched my tits and pressed a finger into my pussy. I kept waiting for her to react, to give some sign that my touch was making an impression. After a while I accepted that she wasn't keen that evening and set my hand on her thigh, squeezing gently while she pushed another thick finger inside me.

"Oh, that's good," I moaned when she went for three. It was a tight fit, but I was so aching and aroused at that point I just wanted more, more, more. I fucked her fingers and the Jacuzzi jet while she filled me and stretched me. Still, the warm gush pounded my clit. It felt harder all the time, like the more turned on I got, the more pressure it blasted me with.

Now it was Danielle's turn to pick up a rose petal and brush it across my skin. It felt so lovely, so velvety soft against my cheek, that I slowed my thrusts for a moment just to concentrate on that beautiful sensation.

When I looked up at my girlfriend, the downy expression on her face made me breathe deeply. "You really are the most beautiful woman in the world," I told her.

I figured she would brush off my compliment as flattery, but when she blushed and said, "Thanks," I wondered if I'd finally convinced her it was true.

When Danielle dragged a rose petal down my chest and then across my tortured tits, the sensation brought a swell of buzzing heat to my pelvis. I felt another orgasm sitting right there, so close to the surface I could almost taste it.

My sexually psychic sweetheart knew just what to do. Still fucking my pussy with her fingers, she bent down and flicked one of my hard nipples with the tip of her tongue. It felt every bit as good as when she did the same to my clit, which was currently being pounded by the Jacuzzi jet.

"Oh god," I groaned, knowing I was right on the edge. "Yeah, baby, suck it."

She moved to the other breast and teased that nipple with her tongue. Even with her lips parted, I could see the grin on her face.

"Suck it!" I growled, pressing the back of her head against my breast.

She turned to look at me, pressing her cheek against my nipple. Her fingers hadn't let up—they were still fucking me impossibly hard, never slowing, though her knuckles rapped against the tub with every blow.

I was so close, so close. The other orgasms were just prep work, just baby orgasms leading up to the mother of all. I bucked against her fingers and the Jacuzzi jet because those were key ingredients, but I knew the second she sucked my tit I would come so hard she'd feel it vicariously.

Bathwater and rose petals lapped against Danielle's face as she watched me flirt with this orgasm. "You want me to suck your tits?" she teased.

"God, yes!"

Without answering, she turned her head softly against my breast. I wasn't sure if it was the sight, the sensation, or just the buildup, but when Danielle wrapped her lips around my nipple, the buzzing weight in my pelvis erupted. The release was like a shimmering heat blasting through my core, warming my heart and body together. I was screaming, moaning, whimpering as Danielle nibbled my tits, fucking my pussy relentlessly...

And then the Jacuzzi timer tick-tick-ticked above my head and, all at once, the jets turned off.

Before the rose petals could stop dancing in the water, I cried, "Turn it on! Turn it on!" and Danielle reached her one unoccupied hand up to bring the wicked tub back to life.

The very second that jet blasted my clit, I soared back into climax, this time higher than before, feeling the heat low in my belly rising, swelling, releasing through my clit. I looked past Danielle's beautiful face to watch her hand pounding my pussy, to watch the invisible power of the jet as it made my lips dance like the petals. God, I was so turned on my clit was nearly the same color as those roses. I knew I couldn't take much more. There was a thin line between pleasure and pain, and I was starting to feel the internal itch that meant pain was close at hand.

My pussy muscles were still milking Danielle's fingers when I crossed that threshold, crying, "Enough, enough! No more, babe."

But she didn't back off, not right away. She swooped me away from the abrasive jet, but replaced it with her thumb, rubbing my clit in circles—hard.

I squirmed and splashed in the tub, screaming now, crying under that heavy sense of "I can't take it anymore" until she kissed me quiet. Slowly, she eased her fingers out of my pussy. Rose-infused bathwater soothed the aching heat between my legs as we writhed together, kissing gently, flesh against flesh.

"Your skin is so soft," I said, though I'd said those words many times before. "I love it. I love the curve at your side, where you rise and fall, where your hips give way to your thighs." I kissed her shoulder and she kissed my neck. "I love your legs. I love your feet. I love your toes. I love you."

"I love you too," she whispered, like she was in a daze. We turned off the jets and rested together inside a ring of rose petals until our fingers were like prunes. And then we got out and dried each other with fluffy white towels.

Danielle turned on the TV, and when I joined her in a bed strewn with rose petals, she was watching Letterman and eating jujubes. There was something impossibly cute about that, and when I snuggled against her bath-warm body, my heart felt too big for my chest. I wanted this feeling—always. No more juvenile insecurities. They'd plagued me from the very start of our relationship, but I was getting tired of being jealous of a memory. We were together, in bed, in love, in life. It was time to grow up. It was well past that time.

Naked and happy, I kissed my girl and she tasted like candy. "Did you have fun in the bath?" I asked her.

"You have no idea," she said with a little laugh. "You'll never believe how much pleasure I get watching you come. It's better than feeling it myself."

"It's better to give than to receive," I replied—that was her motto.

"Exactly," she said, and when I scooped a handful of scarlet petals off the duvet, she took a deep breath and blew them across our bed. My chest filled with warmth as I watched them flutter and fall.

COCKADOODLE DOO

Dawn Mueller

"Any requests?" I ask as I stand by her bed waiting for her to come out of the bathroom.

"Yes," she says definitively. "Enigma."

I should have known. That's become our seduction CD. This particular recording is filled with remixes of the best of Gregorian chants and breathy French lyrics coupled with subtle, yet powerful rhythmic thrusts.

I scroll to the CD on my iPod and hit play. I'm still wearing my winter pajama bottoms and my white tank top, both hanging loosely from my slender, athletic frame, when she emerges from the bathroom. She is in nothing but a black G-string. I still see the faint remnants of a bikini tan around her breasts as she moves in time with the slow, intense groove currently throbbing from the speakers. Her form brings together the best of both worlds to me. Beneath her soft curves lies a body made firm from a disciplined regimen that awes even a stalwart exerciser such as myself.

She approaches me with no hesitation and puts her mouth on mine, hard. Her tongue probes deeply. I feel her teeth around my lips. The sensation of her kisses travels down my spine and into my clit, and I know already that I'm in trouble. She's been in a mood all evening. She is cocky and ready to have her way with me again.

Ever since she figured out how my clit works two days ago, she's been incorrigible (with good reason). After all, in the sixteen or more years that I've been dating women, not one of them has ever taken the time to help me discover what works best for me. I was beginning to get frustrated at the increasingly inordinate amount of time it was taking me to reach orgasm. And the more frustrated I became, the more difficult the orgasm was to reach. In fact, before she took the time to get to know my pussy more intimately, it had become nearly impossible.

Now she strips me of all clothes and pushes me back onto the bed. She's on top of me in a flash, kissing me more insistently than before, her body writhing between my legs. She pushes herself into me by holding on to the headboard with one arm as the music builds in intensity. Her face is a passionate mask of desire, eyes looking out from a place so marked by seduction even she seems surprised to find herself there.

As she had promised when we were curled up in the other room watching the occasionally steamy episodes of *The L Word*, she makes her way down my body with measured patience. She kisses my neck, my nipples, my stomach and my inner thighs, knowing full well that momentum is building within me. I try to touch her, caress her, win her over to my control, but she puts a quick end to my advances by moving my hands away from her every time I try.

When she finally gets down to my pussy, she purposely avoids the one spot that now aches for her, working instead around my lips and above my clit. Her tongue is an expert manipulator and when it plunges unexpectedly into me, my lungs are purged of oxygen by a heavy sigh of pleasure. She stops before going too far, though, because she knows if she gives me too much too soon, I will try to force the orgasm, which is when it retreats.

Instead, she takes a break and props herself up on her knees, looking down at me as I look up at her, eyes wide with desire. She sways seductively to the music. I dare not blink lest I miss any of the show before me. Her hand slides down the front of her G-string and into the warm, moist depths of her freshly shaved pussy. She gyrates slowly against her hand and brings moistened fingertips out and up to her lips. She licks them delicately, as though cleaning her fingers of a particularly decadent dessert. A sucker for desserts, I already know how decadent this particular dish is and long for a taste of it myself. Perhaps sensing my desire, she slides her fingers into herself again, only this time she brings the reward to my lips and allows me to taste it briefly before smearing some of it around my face so I can smell her as she goes back down on me.

I wonder if I'm swollen for her yet or how wet I am. I try not to think about it, but can't help it when I look down at her and see her looking up at me, her face buried deep in my pussy. She is still avoiding my clit and continues to manipulate my lips with her tongue, darting inside me for longer stretches as I feel myself open completely to her. I try to remember to breathe into it and not to force anything. The minute I think I might try to force an orgasm, she stops and moves back out for another break. I worry briefly that the momentum will be lost, but trust now more than ever that she knows exactly what she's doing.

She props herself up on her knees again and slides her hand into the front of her G-string, bringing forth more wetness for me to sample. I imagine myself looking like a wide-eyed kid experiencing some magical wonderland for the very first time. It all feels new to me in so many ways—ways I had all but lost hope of ever experiencing.

Her eyes burn into me when she resumes her position between my legs, and I look back at her before arching myself toward her and moving my pelvis into her tongue. My hand moves to my nipple and I squeeze it gently, then more tightly. I am moaning with pleasure, feeling her move less and less around my clit and more and more toward it.

She doesn't stop for another break, but keeps the momentum at a controlled pace so I don't get too tense or worked up all at once. It is a slow build, one that creeps up on me as I try to breathe through the pleasure and enjoy every last ounce that I can. Her tongue pierces me so deeply that now when it goes inside me and I open for her, I feel like I could come from the inside out. But she too is aware of this and stops again, moving on to lightly graze my clit with her tongue. I feel myself dripping onto the bed. I want it so bad, but am too busy feeling the full experience to force anything. I trust that she knows all too well what to do with my pussy now that she has it tamed.

I lose track of my nipple when she adds a little more pressure and speed to her work with my clit. She doesn't stay in any place too long, though, moving from being inside me back to my clit just before I have a chance to force anything to happen. She continues this pattern, now familiar with when and how the crescendo happens and how to play with my body to take it where it wants to go.

The speed of her tongue increases and I release the tension in my legs to gain the full sensation of what she's doing. Again she moves back inside me, but this time she doesn't stay there long before returning to my clit and remaining there. I feel the start of an orgasm as it builds in the distance, creeping steadily forward. She coaxes it closer with her tongue working double- and triple-time. She knows the end is near just as I do. Instead of forcing it, I wait for it to come slowly, to spread completely as it radiates through my entire body.

"I'm coming!" I announce as though she doesn't already know. "Don't stop!"

She continues what she's doing, not to obey me but because it's what she'd planned on doing anyway. The radiating pleasure now finds a focal point directly beneath her magnificent, patient tongue. I am open and relaxed and I look down at her one more time before the explosive orgasm screams through me and leaves my clit throbbing gently against her face. She continues using her tongue on me, drawing the orgasm out for what seems like an eternity too short.

As the throbbing dies down and my heart rate returns to normal, she lifts herself from between my legs and moves back up to face me, lying once again with her body between my legs. Her face is wet with the fruits of her labor and she rubs it gently against my chin as she kisses me.

Yes, she has good reason to be cocky. Very good reason, indeed.

THREESOME

H.M. Husley

I looked at the clock and knew I'd have to get going soon. Jennifer was expecting me around 8:00 P.M. and it was already 7:30. I still needed to figure out what the hell to wear and, more importantly, how to handle myself. Tonight was not going to be an easy or particularly fun night. It should be, but it wouldn't be. Not with Kat coming to town.

Kat, who symbolized all the things I wasn't and provided Jennifer with the adventure I couldn't. Kat, who had bronze, sun-flecked skin from hours of outdoor soccer practice. Kat, who had lean, capable thighs that pumped like engine pistons, and tight, powerful abs. Kat, who had the kind of body that keeps black-and-white photography in business. Shadows and light caressed her curves, lured the viewer closer and dared hands to reach out and touch her. Kat, who had spent the whole day with Jennifer without me and threatened to steal my girlfriend away.

I tried to put these thoughts out of my mind. It was Jennifer's birthday, and I had agreed to play nice. I splashed water on my face, resolving to make the best of it, and carefully chose the jeans that best accentuated my ass and the shirt that brought out my eyes. Kat might be the flavor of the week but I was still going to let her—and Jennifer—know that there was competition.

I buttoned my shirt, stared at myself in the mirror and admired my finest features. With a smirk on my face I thought, *Maybe this won't be so bad after all.* I took a little extra time fixing my hair, put on cologne and picked out my favorite watch—brushed stainless steel with a white face and bold numbers. The watch always makes the outfit.

At Jennifer's house I parked, killed the engine, closed my eyes and took a deep breath. I stepped out of the car, smoothed the front of my jeans, checked the cuffs of my shirt and straightened my belt. My heart pounded with anticipation and anxiety. The weight of gravity made it feel almost impossible for me to drag one foot in front of the other, but before I knew it, I was pushing the front door open. Jennifer was waiting for me in the foyer and greeted me with a sly grin.

"Hey you! Happy birthday! You look great!" I smiled back at her, my heart beating faster. I looked around nervously for Kat but didn't find her and we moved into the living room. "How was your day? What have you two been up to?"

"It was good," Jennifer said. "We went for a long bike ride down by the creek and had dinner at the Little Cantina. I had this amazing enchilada and Kat loved the fajitas."

"Awesome." I could hear a slight break in my tone.

Before I could ask where she was, Kat came down the stairs and met us near the couch. I was glad that we hadn't sat down yet. "Hey, you must be Kat. I'm Sam. How's it going? How was the drive?" I asked.

"Good, good. The drive wasn't bad and Jennifer and I had a great day!"

There was a slight pause before I could force out a half-hearted "Fantastic!"

"So," Kat asked, "what's up for tonight?"

"Well," I said, "it's Jennifer's birthday, so it's up to her, but I think we should head downtown and check out Spin. It's a mixed crowd but they've got great music and strong drinks. Speaking of which, does anyone want a cocktail?" I wasn't really trying to be hospitable, but my chest was getting tight and I needed something to take the edge off.

"That would be great," Jennifer said.

"Definitely," Kat agreed.

"Good," I said a little too enthusiastically.

When I came back from the kitchen with our drinks, the stereo was playing dance music and Jennifer and Kat were at the dining room table setting up a card game. "It's pretty early, so I decided we should play games," Jennifer said.

"Sure." I set the drinks down. Jennifer loved games and was always playing them. Card games, board games, word games, mind games, love games—all kinds of games.

I sat down and made a healthy start on my drink. I swear to god that was the best drink I have ever had. As soon as the chill of the vodka and the bubbles of the club soda hit my throat, I began to relax.

We made small talk while we played and drank, and Kat somehow started to become less threatening. Maybe it was a full moon, maybe it was the vodka. I don't know. But for some reason I suddenly knew that this would be no ordinary night. I began to look at Kat differently, noticing her lips and her eyes and the way she brushed her hair out of her face. When the music stopped I sat quietly for a moment before suggesting we head out. "Hey guys, should we get to the bar?"

"Sure, we can take my car if you want," offered Kat.

"Wait," I said, "is that BMW out there yours?"

"Yeah. You wanna drive?"

Did I want to drive? Was she kidding? That car was like sex on wheels. Of course I wanted to drive! "Sure," I replied nonchalantly.

Kat handed me the keys and we moved toward the door. Jennifer must have seen the gleam in my eye because she put her arm around me and whispered in my ear, "Well, someone sure perked up! I told you you'd like her." I could only grin as I swung my arm around Jennifer's waist and kissed her softly on the cheek. I unlocked the car, opened the door, and slid onto the black leather seat.

"I'll let you two ride up front," I heard Jennifer say. I had to take a moment to appreciate the beauty of the machine in my hands before I could start the engine. Black on black, loaded, six speed gearbox. This car was made to be driven, and I was definitely in the mood to drive. I put the key in the ignition and looked over at Kat. "Are you sure you wanna do this?"

"Go for it!" she said.

It was nearly all freeway between Jennifer's place and the club, and this detail was not lost on me. I started the engine and peeled out into the road, cautious at first, a little overwhelmed by the power.

"I know you know how to drive this beast better than that," taunted Kat.

"Definitely," I said as we turned onto the freeway entrance ramp.

I shoved the clutch down and put the car into third gear to accelerate. When I let up on the clutch and pushed the accelerator down I could feel the raw energy of the motor in my thighs. When we hit fourth gear and 60 miles per hour I could feel it in my arms. In fifth gear at 70 miles per hour I could feel it in my stomach.

"Go ahead," said Kat, "take it to sixth." I weaved in and out of traffic, approaching 85 miles per hour. Now I could feel it in my clit. Kat and Jennifer could see it on my face.

I'm not sure how long it really took us to get downtown, but it felt like it was over before it began. As we walked toward the club I could still feel the revving of the engine coursing through my veins. I walked in between Jennifer and Kat with an arm around each of them and held them close.

When we got inside I led the girls to the dance floor, where the thumping of the bass overwhelmed my senses. Everything melted into the beat and my mind completely shut off. The club was packed, the energy high, the strobes pulsing, the drinks flowing, and the three of us moved together as one. The rhythms and cadences of the music captivated our bodies and propelled us toward one another. Without thinking I pulled Kat closer and kissed her. She tasted like cherries and her lips were like cashmere. I looked over at Jennifer and she was just smiling, so I kissed her, too. I'd never done anything quite like this before. It's probably a good thing I didn't have time to think about it. Kat grabbed my ass while I kissed Jennifer, and it was all I could do to stay on my feet. Everything felt electric.

We'd only been at the club for an hour or so when Jennifer pulled me aside and said, "Let's go home. I want to show you what I really want for my birthday." Then she turned to Kat and said, "You don't mind if we go home early, do you?" Before Kat could respond Jennifer kissed her roughly, then softly on the mouth. Then she took both of us by the hand and we followed her out onto the street.

"I'm not sure if I can drive," I said.

"Baby, you can drive," Jennifer said, "I won't have it any other way." Kat and I looked at each other in agreement and nodded at Jennifer. It wasn't that I'd had too much to drink. I just wasn't sure I could slow the shaking in my legs enough to control the car.

My ears were still ringing and my legs were still quivering when we got back to the house. I'd hardly caught my breath when Jennifer pointed to Kat and me and said, "You and you. In my bed. Now." She followed us to the bedroom, made sure we did as we were told and left, shutting the door behind her.

Kat and I looked at each other with some combination of confusion and lust. "Is she coming back?" Kat asked.

"Does it matter?" I replied.

"I guess it doesn't." Kat pushed me down on the bed and straddled me. She ran her mouth along my neck, my jaw, my lips, coming so close to my skin that I thought she touched me even though she didn't. I lifted myself slightly off the bed in pursuit of her lips, but she just pushed me down again.

"I know what you like," she said.

"Oh really..." I started to say. But then she put her finger on my lips.

"Shh. Less talking and more listening." Kat ran her hands along my body, pausing to pay special attention to my hips and the outer curves of my breasts. She started to tug at my shirt with her teeth when the door opened.

"What do you two think you're doing?" Jennifer asked tauntingly.

"We're, uh, we were just—" I stammered.

"Who said you could talk?" interrupted Jennifer. Kat and I fell silent as Jennifer began to undress. First she slipped off her top, seductively pushing each strap off her shoulders and then letting the rest of the garment fall to the floor. She was wearing one of those expensive Victoria's Secret bras with black lace and a little extra lift to augment her breasts.

"Kat," she commanded, "come unhook my bra." Kat obediently obliged as I sat watching, stupefied. "Now take off Sam's shirt, but don't touch!" Jennifer continued. "That's good. Now take off your shirt. Then I want to watch you undress her." Without realizing it I had started to breathe heavily. "We're just getting started, Sam, you should relax."

I swallowed hard and Kat continued to remove my clothing. After my shirt she took off my bra, my belt, and my pants. As I lay there in my boxers I didn't know what to think, but before I could contemplate my fate too much Jennifer pulled Kat off the bed and kissed her hard, pulling her hair with one hand and squeezing her ass with the other.

"You know what I want, don't you?" Jennifer asked me. I shook my head. "Come on, baby," she said. "You know exactly what I want." My heart pounded because I did know. Kat looked on, smiling. "I've got plans for you, too," said Jennifer as she pushed Kat back down on the bed. "You can start by kissing my girl, but not on the lips. Show me how much you appreciate her body," she demanded.

Kat did as she was told while Jennifer watched. She moved from my neck to my collarbone to my shoulder and then down the center of my chest, giving me soft kisses and flicking her tongue. When Kat got to my hips and my pelvis, she lingered near my groin and then turned me over, nipping and biting the small of my back first, then moving down my ass to the back of my thighs. My entire body was hot, burning from the inside out.

Before Kat could turn me back over I heard Jennifer's voice. "That's good. Now cover her eyes with this bandana and then put this on." I felt Kat pull away from me, taking the heat with her. "And you," Jennifer said to me, "don't move." Kat sat on top of me and tied the bandana around my head. When she got up I heard some rustling and waited impatiently. While Kat adjusted the strap-on, Jennifer got into bed and rolled me onto my side. She pressed her naked body against mine and wrapped her arms around me so she could play with my nipples, pinching, pulling and rubbing. When she knew I was getting desperate she moved from my breasts to my side, caressing me gently, making me wait. I let out a moan and Jennifer bit my neck, bringing me back to the edge.

My mind was completely void of coherence when Jennifer got up and rolled me onto my back. "Your turn," she said to Kat. I felt Kat's hands on my thighs and sat up to kiss her. "No one told you to move," said Jennifer. I smiled broadly and lay back down while Kat ran her fingertips along the inside of my thighs. She moved slowly and worked her way up to my cunt, letting her fingers graze my lips and my clit. I wanted to press my body into her hand but knew better than to move before I was told.

Kat continued to tease me, and it felt like she would never give me what I wanted. My pussy was hot, swollen and dripping. I could feel the blood push against my skin from the inside as my clit pulsed. Finally Kat pushed my legs open and let me feel the head of her cock on my cunt. She moved it in slow circles and then up and down while Jennifer kissed me and squeezed my tits. I put my hands on Kat's thighs and dug my nails into her skin, silently begging her to enter me. When she did I gasped and held my breath. "That's it, baby," Jennifer whispered. "Just let it go."

As Kat thrust into me slowly and deeply I could feel my body clinging to her cock, squeezing it and clenching around it. She moved so smoothly, so forcefully. I still wanted more, and Jennifer gave it to me. Kneeling above me, she taunted my lips with her cunt while Kat continued to fuck me. I grabbed Jennifer by the hips and pulled her into me. She didn't resist and I hungrily took her into my mouth.

Kat started moving faster. I followed her pace as I licked and sucked Jennifer's clit, pausing every now and then to pay attention to her lips and sink my tongue inside her. Jennifer started breathing hard and Kat pulled her in for a kiss. We moved together, our bodies completely entwined. Pumping, grinding, stroking. Jennifer pushed herself into me, rocking back and forth as Kat did the same to me. Sweat beaded up on my skin and ran down my face. My jaw started to ache and my hands were sore from clutching the sides of the bed. My heart pounded so hard I thought it would burst.

Suddenly Jennifer stopped moving and held herself firmly above me. I heard her hold her breath and then let out a guttural moan before she lay down next to me. I tried to catch my own breath but Kat was moving faster still. The pleasure was almost too much. I sat up and wrapped my body around Kat as she continued to move. When my nails tore the skin on her back she knew to stay still until it was over, leaving my body trembling. Kat kissed me softly as Jennifer held me and said, "See? You always know what I want." I let out a deep sigh, smiled, let my body sink into the mattress and reveled in the sheer ecstasy of complete satisfaction—without a trace of jealousy.

DELINQUENTS

Catherine Paulssen

It was the summer of 1994.

I didn't know it then, but that would be the best summer of my life. Britpop would hit the German radio stations and give us the feeling that we could be just as rebellious and quixotic as we imagined our parents had been when the Beatles were young. Bitten by the soccer bug, we would cheer our national team on all the way to the quarterfinals. "Beverly Hills 90210" would still be fresh and Janet Jackson would educate us about sensuality. We were sweet sixteen and could officially order alcohol. The days were long, bright and full of promise.

Esther and I were spending the summer vacation house-sitting her mom's four-bedroom crib while she was out of the country working on location. The house was decorated exactly as one would expect of a well-paid TV actress in her late thirties with an only child and no distinct taste of her own: its fashionable elegance was straight out of a design catalogue and always presentable in case a magazine asked to do a home story.

Esther's mom was away a lot, so I stayed over a lot—so often, in fact, that I knew my way around the house in the dark and almost considered it a second home. At Esther's place, we did all the things we usually weren't allowed to do, at least not at my parents' house. It was a different world.

The July days were hot, and we were lazy. In a mere two days, we had transformed the picture-perfect space into a sight that could be no longer considered home story material. That second night, after we had tried on all of her mom's fancy heels, the extravagant, expensive ones that you only eye longingly in a store window, Esther suggested we do makeovers.

"My mom got this kit from Helena Rubinstein to try out, you know, since they're using it on her show and she might do commercials."

After my embarrassing performance trying to walk in a woman's shoes, I wasn't very keen on further attempts to look glamorous. In fact, all I wanted was to slump on that huge sofa in the living room, order takeout and watch TV. "I don't know," I said, wrinkling my nose.

"Kitty, come on, it'll be fun!" said Esther, reaching for one of the perfume bottles on her mom's vanity table and spritzing something on me that smelled like Christmas in an Oriental bazaar. "We'll backcomb and make our hair big, like they had in the sixties! Or we'll do curls."

"I already have curls," I said dryly, but she ran into the bathroom and returned with a box.

"Real curls," she stated, taking out a set of curlers. I had doubts they would even stick in my shoulder-length hair, but Esther insisted. Soon we looked like two quintessential suburban housewives getting ready to hit the town.

"How long do they need to stay in?" I asked, already loathing the scratchy things that tweaked my hairline.

"Until the hair is dry." Esther fixed the curlers with a hair spray whose scent made me feel as though I'd just walked out of a hair salon. I watched her face in the bathroom mirror. Whereas my reflection made it clear that I was only experimenting with lipstick and eye shadow, Esther looked truly alluring. She was beautiful anyway, but the soft pink lip gloss and thick mascara that made her big eyes look even bigger added to the natural glow I'd always envied.

"You look really good," I said.

She tilted her head and grinned. "We're two hotties," she said, giving me a short squeeze and miming a kiss toward the mirror. "Come on, let's order pizza and see what's on TV."

"Get us some wine!" said Esther, flashing a mischievous glance at me before answering the doorbell. I picked a bottle of white wine that had a golden castle drawn on its label. It looked nice to me, but I had no clue if it was wine you could get in a supermarket or an expensive bottle from some noble winery that Esther's mom had gotten from an admirer. I opened it anyway. I never got the feeling that she cared much about what went on in her house.

"Do you feel as hot as I do?" Esther asked, picking pieces of salami off the last slice of pizza. I threw a glance at her flushed cheeks and nodded. She opened the French door to the garden, and even though the air that breezed into the living room now was lukewarm, it felt like a cool draft to me. A half glass of wine had been enough to make me dizzy. From her spot at the garden door, Esther watched me zap through the TV channels.

"Uh, stay there!" she ordered when I landed on the opening credits of a thriller.

I don't remember what the movie was about, only that its

horror was more psychological than gory—so much so that we were already creeped out a mere thirty minutes in.

"Turn it off! Turn it off!" Esther shrieked when a pitch-black shadow appeared out of nowhere on screen.

I pushed the button, and darkness fell over the living room.

"I will never leave this chair again," she said, and pulled her knees up to her chin.

Both of us turned to look at the half-opened garden door. "Rock, paper, scissors?" I suggested, and lost. When I returned, Esther had snuggled into my seat on the sofa.

I raised an eyebrow. "And I thought you were going to live in the armchair from now on."

"Very funny," she said, making a face. "You're scared too."

"At least I went to shut the doors."

"Only because you lost!"

"Chicken."

"Takes one to know one."

I laughed. "You don't even dare sit on the dark side of the living room!"

"Well, your silhouette looked really scary from over there."

I turned and caught a glimpse of my shadow. My head looked distorted against the naked walls, and the curlers made it look three times as big. "Point taken."

"I can't go to bed now," she complained. "Can you get us a video out?"

I rolled my eyes but went over to the shelf and scanned the rows of purchased tapes and those Esther had recorded from television, all labeled in her slanted, dynamic handwriting. "*Dirty Dancing?*"

Esther puffed. "Not again."

"What's this one? Kylie Minogue?" I picked up a tape that said *The Delinquents* on the cover.

"They're this small-town couple in the fifties, and their parents won't let them be together because they're underage. It's good, let's watch it."

I immediately loved Lola, Kylie Minogue's character. She must have been around my age, but she knew what she wanted and she broke all the rules to get it once she had made up her mind. I wished I could be that rebellious. I wished I could find such a star-crossed love and be happy and wistful all the time.

"I wonder if it's true," Esther mused, her eyes glued to the screen. "I mean, if sex is really that great."

I shrugged. "Don't know. But when Julian got under my shirt, it felt pretty awkward."

Esther snorted. "That's because Julian is a jerk!" I snickered. "But it must be better than that," she said, a note of defiance in her tone. "I once saw my mom doing it."

My eyes widened. "You walked in on your mom?"

"You can't tell anyone!"

I shook my head. "Cross my heart."

"It was with one of the camera guys."

"Weren't they mad at you?"

"I don't think they saw me. I backtracked immediately. And they were too caught up... Well, actually, my mom was wearing a blindfold and he was...busy."

"A blindfold?" I whispered, breath bated. "And what was he doing?"

Esther was silent for a moment. "He had his head between... her boobs and he kissed them and licked them and, you know. What guys do."

"I can't imagine what the fuss is all about. I mean, what's with the boob obsession?"

Esther threw a glance at the movie and shrugged. "Don't know. They must feel good, I guess."

"Maybe," I said, following Esther's stare. But then, suddenly, she turned her eyes from the screen and looked right at me.

"Wanna try?" she asked.

Heat shot into my stomach. I knew immediately what she meant. But it seemed too outrageous a suggestion. And what was I supposed to do? What if I did it all wrong? What if it was embarrassing? I kept my eyes fixed on the television. "Try what?" I asked.

She cocked her head, but didn't answer my question. "To see if it feels good," she stated simply.

My hands grew sweaty. "How... I mean, do you... Are you serious?" I knew she was. I could always tell when Esther was serious.

She averted her eyes and fiddled with the waistband of her pajamas. "Just...to find out. I mean, we could see what it feels like."

I swallowed and looked at her *Pretty Woman* T-shirt, washed so many times the letters were barely visible. Not that I wasn't curious. But not as curious as I was scared. I turned back to the screen. I could never imagine being like that with a man. The one thing I could relate to was the clumsiness with which Brownie, Lola's boyfriend, undressed her. But Esther... I had known her since forever. She had been my one true confidante, no matter what. Still...

"Don't you think it will be strange?" I asked.

She kept her gaze fixed on the couch. "No," she said, and even though her voice was small, there was no doubt in it. Somehow, her confidence rubbed off on me and compounded my curiosity.

"Okay."

She raised her head. "Yes?"

I nodded. For a moment, we looked at each other as if we

were mountaineers, steeling ourselves before climbing some unknown, hazardous mountain. A serene earnestness descended over Esther's face. "Count to three?" she asked, and again I nodded.

We counted and stripped the shirts off our bodies.

I had seen her breasts before—while trying on bras together, giggling and making fun of each other in the changing cubicle until an annoyed shop assistant told us to keep it down. This time, it was different. It wasn't the casual glance you throw at another girl's breasts in the locker room to see if they already look more like a grown woman's breasts than yours. If they are bigger. Better shaped. More attractive.

This time, I took in her breasts. Before I could even think of actually touching them with my hands—to touch them with my lips seemed so shockingly unimaginable, I could barely wrap my head around the thought—I explored them with my eyes.

Esther's breasts were like two parts of a small apple, cute and a bit uneven. The bluish light that flickered from the TV made her skin appear even paler than it already was. Her nipples were tiny and pink.

I was so lost in contemplation of her breasts that her sudden touch on my own breasts startled me. Her hands were cold. They were always cold. Then, as my nipples contracted at the chilly brush, she bent down and tentatively licked my breast.

The sensations that shot through me at that moment were so overwhelming, they didn't leave room for thought, they didn't leave room for doubt—they didn't leave room for any confusion but the one they caused. I felt as though I were being poked by a thousand small flames. They bit me and stung me and wandered over my whole body like galvanic fireflies. My mind went blank, my breath hitched in my throat.

Esther pressed her lips against my nipple and started to suck at it very gently. It felt better than anything I had ever experienced before. I became nothing but nerves and cells that were vibrating and dancing and passing the joy from my breast to the farthest parts of my body. Nothing existed but her tongue on my skin. It was as if her mouth were caressing my whole body. I became this tiny person swept away by her tongue.

Nonetheless, I wanted more. Each swipe was the revelation of some unnamed longing I didn't even know I had, and it made me want more. A hollow feeling crept up from my belly at the thought that maybe she wouldn't be able to give it to me. At each kiss, at each suck of my nipple, I wanted to take her, shake her, press her head closer to me, closer to my body. I wanted to make her do more, lick at me again, never stop.

Her lips stumbled over my body, showering my breasts with kisses, traveling down to my navel, gracing every part of my naked skin. Her nose tickled my belly, and she placed her hands around my hips. They felt even colder on my skin than they had before. Or maybe they were just as cold, only my body had become feverish.

I glanced down at my breasts, and all of a sudden, they looked beautiful. I had never been too satisfied with their shape when I was sitting up. They weren't molded as I felt they should be. But now that Esther was treating them so tenderly, they had formed into graceful curves, like very round-bellied pearls. Their tips pointed at Esther's lips, shivering for the attention of her warm, loving tongue.

It felt as if she were feeding on how deeply she had overwhelmed me. The more I sighed and the more breathless pleas I uttered, the more devotedly she caressed me. I leaned back against the sofa and forgot all my questions, forgot even the curlers in my hair.

With a pant, Esther eventually stopped. She sat up, and the

look she gave me was almost wild. "Show me what it feels like. Please."

I pushed her gently into the cushions. She extended her arms over her head, and her body shone in the TV's cold light like that of a porcelain doll. It was the most beautiful sight I had ever seen. Her slightly stretched breasts, the oval hollow of her belly button, her contracted nipples and the dark skin around them covered in chills—was she cold? Aroused? Ambivalent? As much as I wanted to touch her, I felt I could easily go hours simply watching her.

In the end, the stare in her eyes—shy, dark, excited, trusting—chased away whatever last inhibitions I had. She clasped her fingers together and sank her head a little lower into the cushions. The rosy tips of her nipples stood out against the paleness like decorations on a birthday cake, one you hadn't expected to get, one just waiting for you to dip your fingers into its frothy surface, lick at the sweet, thick cream, let it melt on your tongue and fill your mouth with an anticipation and craving that would be appeased only when your teeth finally sank into the cake itself.

I placed a trail of kisses between her breasts. Maybe I was too self-conscious to start licking at them right away. Maybe, as one does with a birthday cake, I wanted to save the best for last.

Esther arched her back and poked one of her nipples against my cheek. A little sigh escaped her lips as the hard nub brushed my skin, and a tremor of glee ran through me as I realized how much more pleasure I would be able to give her if I just turned my head a little, just closed my lips around the tip of her breast, just sucked it into my mouth. The ripples of Esther's caress still vibrated deep within me; to know I would be able to lift her to the same heights of longing and revelation and fulfillment was nothing short of elation.

I rested my hand on her breast and my chin on her belly. With slow moves of my finger, I drew a circle around her nipple. I traced the dark patch until Esther's choked sighs had become impatient whimpers. Finally, I puckered my lips and kissed the underside of her breast. I waited for her astonished moan. I let another kiss follow, this time closer to her nipple. My nose touched the powdery, wrinkled skin, and I rubbed against it for one long, drawn-out moment before kissing it. Esther drew a sharp breath between clenched teeth.

"Oh, how wonderful that is!" she sighed as my lips touched her flesh. "Oh, Kitty, how wonderful that is!"

I buried my lips hungrily in her flesh, took in as much of her as I could and watched her breast glisten in the twilight before bending down again and licking at her warm, damp skin. I couldn't remember why sucking on them had ever seemed outlandish. Now it was the only thing I wanted to do, the only thing that felt right or natural. I enclosed the hard nub with my lips and gently sucked it into my mouth. Esther let out a little cry, a very high-pitched moan, and her knuckles became white as her hands clutched the sofa cushions.

I knew she was melting and at the same time consumed by undefined yearning. I kissed her creamy skin and luscious nipples, mine for the taking, while on screen, Eddie Cochran sang about steps one, two and three to heaven.

I couldn't tell how long I loved her. It might have been hours, it might have been a few blissful minutes. All I knew was that it hadn't been long enough. In an attempt to push me closer onto her breasts, Esther pressed her hands against my neck. The heavenly soft feeling of her smooth flesh in my mouth was pierced by a sting of pain as she pushed one of the curlers into my scalp. I turned my head a bit to escape the pressure of her hands and scratched her tender nipple with a loosening curler.

"Ouch," she hissed and drew her hand over her breast.

We looked at each other and the thought hit me that usually, we would have broken into wild giggles over something like that. Now, though, neither of us laughed. And that made me feel like crying. I retreated a bit and suddenly noticed how cold I had become.

Esther propped herself up onto her elbows. "Maybe we should go to sleep."

As quietly as she did, I reached for my pajama shirt. We didn't say a word as we walked upstairs, and without another look at her, I vanished into the bathroom.

I took the curlers out of my hair and regarded the effect in the mirror. My hair sprang in glossy curls off my shoulders, and I liked the way they framed my face so sophisticatedly. I felt incredibly grown-up. When I looked at my reflection— cheeks still a bit flushed, eyes filled with a shimmer I hadn't seen before—I could tell even then that I had found something tonight that would lead me a step closer to who I was.

A few minutes later, as I lay in the spare bed that had been set up in the corner of Esther's room, the intoxicating feeling of maturity was gone. I felt helpless and confused and at a loss about how we would act the next morning.

More than that, I felt we had begun something and not finished it.

I could tell Esther wasn't sleeping either. It haunted me not to know whether she was kept awake by the same bewildering thoughts or by a sense of shame or repulsion.

"Kitty?" she finally asked, breaking the silence.

"Hmm?"

"I can't get that movie out of my head."

I propped my head up onto my hand. "You mean the horror movie?"

"Uh-huh. You think the little kid in the attic survived?"

"Of course she survived."

She rustled her sheet. "That's what I think too."

For some minutes, I heard nothing but a car being parked on the street in front of the house and some late-night bird chatter in the garden.

She finally spoke again. "Kitty?"

"Yes."

She didn't say anything. I lay under the sheets and held my breath. "Can I come sleep in your bed?"

I still didn't breathe. "Yes," I finally managed. I listened to her tiptoeing across the floor. She slipped under my sheet, and the temperature immediately rose.

"Thanks."

I didn't answer.

"Do you still think—"

"Stop talking about that movie!" I interrupted her, more irritated than was fair.

She turned toward me. I could feel her eyes on my face. "No, I mean...do you still think about this?" She laid her hand on my breast.

I sucked my bottom lip into my mouth. The heat in my belly flared up again, as though thousands of ants were crawling through my veins.

"Do you?"

All I could do was nod.

"Me too." She turned her face back toward the ceiling, but her hand remained where it was. "I never imagined it would be possible to feel something like that."

My body urged me to say something meaningful, something

that would make her keep her hand where it was or maybe even move it under my shirt, something that wouldn't sound trite when remembered tomorrow. But I was like the Little Mermaid in the fairy tale: I had gotten my wish but lost my voice. If I claimed it back, maybe the wish would be gone as well?

"Would you... Do you want to do it again?" Esther asked.

Happiness rushed through me. I didn't have to think twice. But... Where would it lead? Would we still be friends after tonight? She stiffened next to me. I realized how much it must have cost her to ask me that question. And how thankful I was that she had.

I nodded.

Esther relaxed. So did I. She sat up and stripped off her shirt. Her body shimmered like a ghost's in the little light that shone in from outside, but it was impossible to make out its contours. I got out of my shirt without really moving much. For a moment, I considered turning on a light because it nagged me that though I would get to feel her breasts once again, I wouldn't get to see them. But as her hand fumbled for my body and her cold fingers found my nipple, the excitement of not knowing what she would do next—where her hands would fondle me, where her lips would kiss me—was even more sizzling. Every touch of her nimble fingers, every tender tweak of my rigid nipples shot right between my legs. The curtain of her hair brushed my chin. I smelled the expensive hair spray as the sleek strands tickled my skin.

A moment later, all that was gone: the only thing that existed was her lips on my skin, the warm touch of her tongue as she carefully licked at my nipple. I threw back my head. She sucked at my nipples and flicked her tongue over them with such patience and devotion that the beating of my pulse between my legs became so hard I had to rub my thighs together in the hopes that my pant seam would provide some relief—or more stimulation.

"Kitty?"

I didn't answer but panted some affirmation to signal she had my fullest attention.

"Can I kiss you?"

I reached out in the dark and brushed her hair behind her ear. My fingers stroked her back. My yes was more a breath than a word, but it was enough for Esther.

She bent me over into the pillow, and a whiff of her toothpaste hit my nose before her breath brushed my lips and erased every other sensation. Our kiss was like all the kisses of two people who think they know everything about each other and then discover an emotion so big, so overwhelming, it can take their relationship to a whole new level—or destroy it.

When Esther kissed me, I knew right away that we would not be destroyed. It was a kiss that was a new beginning, a kiss that transformed our friendship and turned it into something even deeper.

Her naked breasts rubbed against mine. She moaned into my mouth. The throbbing down below had become so strong I couldn't keep the desire to myself any longer. I wanted her badly and most of all, I wanted to show her that want.

I rolled her over, pressed another kiss onto her mouth and moved my hand down her body to the rim of her pajama pants and underneath them. I circled my fingers over her skin and touched the outline of the smooth curls beneath her underpants. She pressed her finger between her teeth but didn't object. I took the finger from her mouth, kissed it and led her hand underneath her panties. I don't know where I got the courage, but it seemed easy at the moment. I looked at her, and she nodded.

"Yes?"

She nodded again. "Yes, please." Underneath me, she spread her legs.

Slowly, my fingers made their way over the rising curve of her pussy and down to the slick folds, warm and somehow vulnerable.

She was wet. So wet. So wet that with one sweep of my hand, I had soaked the tuff of hair and could feel small drops glistening in its tangles. I could have lost myself in the sheer pureness of it, but Esther guided my hand and pressed my finger onto her clit.

"Oh, Kitty..."

I rubbed her up and down, circling the heated skin. Blood raged in my ears as she began to writhe harder and harder. I slid the whole length of my finger between her pussy lips, letting her moans be my guide.

"Yes..." she breathed, and I tried to steady her, tried to keep my finger where she wanted it to be. She squirmed and arched her body, kneaded the sheets with her fist and then dug her fingers into my back.

"Oh, don't stop, Kitty, please don't..." Her body twisted around me as she whimpered in a voice I had never heard before. I gave up my attempts at control and just tried to find her rhythm.

"Yes!" she growled. Again and again, she called out that one word before her voice eventually faded into a string of endearing moans. Like a shell, her pussy closed, and Esther's body came down. She purred one last time, long and relishing, then wrapped her arms around me.

"Oh, Kitty, you have no idea," she exhaled.

She snuggled her body against mine, and her fingertip parted my lips. "Warm it," she demanded, and I sucked at her finger, the sound of her satisfied giggle in my ear. She placed a loud kiss on my cheek and the next moment, her wet finger gently breached the entrance of my pussy.

I bit my bottom lip and moaned with joy when her finger pressed with cautious force against the spot where the throbbing was strongest.

It was the summer of 1994.

RISKING IT ALL

Lynette Mae

My shift finally ended. I turned the corner onto our street, exhausted, sweaty and numb from hours of stress. It was the kind of night that tests the mettle of everyone who has ever donned a uniform and balanced duty and devotion for the public good. That's not to say cops are saints, and I know we're far from perfect, but I'd like to think that it's true what they say about law enforcement. It's a calling.

It had been a night like no other. I've taken more risks than I can count over the years, chased criminals at hair-raising speed, run toward gunfire rather than away and engaged the evils of humanity without much thought. But on this night I'd been tested professionally and personally in ways I could not have imagined before. My emotions were pushed to the breaking point. Thankfully, it was over now. But it wouldn't really be over until we were both home.

The last time I talked to you was when the radio call came in.

We had just finished having dinner together, a treat we rarely allow ourselves because you always say people will talk. I say, "Screw them," and you just shake your head at me. We leaned against the bumpers of our cars and recited our normal give and take.

"I love you."

"More." You smiled that special smile that never fails to set my heart tripping in my chest.

Suddenly, the horrific transmission silenced our playful banter. A bloodcurdling scream from the police radio raised every hair on my body. "Oscar Four! I've been shot!"

Every nerve ending sprang to high alert as voices demanded his location. We jumped into our cars, instinctively heading toward the east end of town, where the Oscar squad worked. You peeled out of the lot just ahead of me, your hand out the window making the *I love you* sign. And then instead of lovers we were two cops, lights flashing and sirens blaring through the city. In the next seconds, responding officers' excited chatter and supervisors shouting for an ambulance mixed with the sounds of the wounded officer's cries over the radio. We pushed our vehicles to the limits, screaming through the streets heedless of our own safety. This was different. One of *us* was down. We needed no official declaration. The manhunt was on.

A minute and a half later we arrived in the area. EMS administered first aid to the injured officer and a ring of uniforms surrounded the scene. The rest of us began to scour the surrounding area for the suspect: a white male last seen driving an older-model Ford truck, orange with a white stripe down the side. "That thing should stick out like a whore in church," I told the cop on scene who gave us the description. I only hoped the bad guy hadn't been able to reach the interstate. I wanted to catch him and I wanted to catch him now.

We fanned out across the sector with our fellow officers, each with our private thoughts for our fallen comrade as we searched. Every cop in the city was in this zone. This guy had to turn up. The helicopter was in the air, checking beyond the immediate grid, just in case he'd gotten farther than we'd anticipated. We were updated regularly with tips and possible sightings, but nothing seemed to be panning out as the hours dragged on. The wounded officer was holding on, and his strength bolstered our resolve.

Finally, around two A.M. a gas station clerk called to say a truck matching the description had just pulled in behind his business. I was four blocks away. I stood on the accelerator and wished for a rocket booster that would get me there faster. My approach was from the west and I immediately saw the rear quarter panel of the truck as I made the corner past the building. Orange paint sent adrenaline surging through my veins. This is the moment cops dream of. With no time to think about anything but preventing escape, I swung my car around to block the suspect vehicle. Another squad car entered the parking lot from the east and we drove our bumpers simultaneously into our target, pinning it there.

I hit the release button on my assault rifle as I threw open the door and launched from my driver's seat toward the car, leading with my muzzle. I moved swiftly to a position just behind the driver's door. In my peripheral vision I could see the other officer approaching the passenger side. The suspect leaned across the bench seat in that direction. Tunnel vision took over, my focus like a laser beam on the driver. The suspect's right arm came up.

"Gun!" the other officer shouted. The world around me exploded in gunfire and flying glass. The popping sound of a pistol and the discharge of my rifle seemed to happen in slow motion. I swear I could see the spent casings ejecting from the port. I fired three times. The suspect jerked each time our bullets struck him. When the firing stopped, my ears were ringing. I was standing at the driver's window looking at the suspect sprawled inside the cab, his right arm outstretched and a pistol just beyond it on the seat. Shards of glass covered everything, including me. I raised my eyes, looking across the interior to where the second officer stood.

"Dana?"

"Holy shit!" I breathed.

You were standing there much as I was, glass clinging to your hair and clothes, tiny cuts on your face and arms. I gulped audibly just before a wave of nausea rolled through my gut, and tried not to think about how this might have turned out. The stunned expression on your face said you were having the same thoughts about me. Neither of us moved. We just blinked and stared. I saw the love in your eyes, but it was fear beneath the surface that twisted my heart. I opened my mouth to speak and nothing came out. The gravity of what had nearly happened overwhelmed me. What if... I cut my eyes to the ground, unable to cope. Service and sacrifice had taken on a whole new dimension.

A flood of officers descended on the location, and controlled chaos erupted around us as the parking lot became posted as a crime scene. Yellow police tape cordoned off the area, investigators swarmed, flashbulbs popped and bullet casings were marked on the blacktop. Each of us was whisked away in a different direction, sequestered pending questioning by detectives and union reps. At headquarters, every once in a while I'd catch a glimpse of you as we moved through different stages of the process. I knew rationally that policy and protocol required us to be separated, but I wanted to see you.

No. I wanted to hold you.

Sometime in those next hours you left a message on my cell that you took a few stitches, but were fine. "See ya later," you started to end, with your standard cheerfulness, and I pictured your dazzling trademark smile. Then I heard you pull in a shaking breath. "I love you, Dana." I closed my eyes and absorbed the tenderness in your voice. Even in the direst of circumstances you give me what I need, and I'm certain I'm not deserving.

At nearly four A.M. I pulled into the drive, longing for the sanctuary of home, our comfortable bed and you. I stripped off my uniform as I moved deliberately through the shadows of the house. The release of the Velcro on my duty belt and the straps on the body armor made sharp noises in the otherwise still darkness, while the chill of the air-conditioning began to ease the fire beneath my skin. Once the layers of work attire and finally my underwear had been shed, I walked nude across the living room, slid open the patio door and stepped onto the lanai. The night air was still thick, hot and sticky.

I silently descended the three stairs into the pool and submerged myself in the crystal water. Cool, liquid relief suffused my overheated body. The light from the full moon overhead and the soft glow of the garden lighting beyond the screen enclosure were the only illumination in the otherwise dark backyard. I dipped under, pushed off from the side wall and crossed the length underwater to surface at the other end. The chill of the water penetrated my body's core, exhilarating and soothing at once. I turned onto my back and floated weightlessly, allowing the peaceful comfort of home to ease the insanity of our shift. I completed another noiseless lap, reveling in the sensation of the water flowing over every inch of my skin. The water muffled all sound to wrap me in fluid quiet, suspending me in its alternate peaceful reality.

I popped up in the shadows at the far end of the pool, suddenly aware of eyes on me. My gaze tracked toward the patio doors to find you standing on the threshold, silhouetted in the light from the house, watching me in the water. Our eyes met across the humid night. A knot of desire twisted in my stomach as you stepped onto the deck, your face intensely focused, staring. Your lips turned up into a soft, sultry smile, a mixture of gratitude and hunger. I opened my mouth to ask you how you were, but the smoldering look in your eyes stole the air from my lungs and the words died on my lips.

Wordlessly, you dropped your gun belt and removed your outer uniform shirt, ballistic vest and T-shirt, exposing your high, firm breasts and sleek torso in the moonlight. My breath caught in my chest. Heaviness in the pit of my stomach quickly spread between my legs, making it difficult to tread water. I crossed to the built-in seat along the wall in the deep end of the pool, bringing me closer to the side, closer to where you stood in just your BDU pants and boots.

When you bent over to untie your boots, your breasts swayed slightly as you worked the laces free. I felt light-headed. You kicked off the boots and socks, unfastened your belt. I stared as you slid your pants down over your hips to your ankles and stepped free. My breathing came faster now as I took in every inch of your well-muscled, beautiful form. Wetness seeped between my legs that had nothing to do with the water in the pool, and my nipples tightened with desire at the sight of you standing before me so beautiful and proud in the moonlight.

You smiled knowingly and eased into the water beside me, settling on the step. I took your hand to pull you onto my lap. Your legs snaked around my waist and I reached out to grab your ass and nestled you tightly against my stomach.

A bandage covered the area on your forehead just above

your left eyebrow. I touched a finger tentatively just at the edge of the gauze. "Can I see?" You nodded and I carefully lifted the tape and the bandage, revealing a line of sutures beneath. "Sorry." I lightly touched my lips to the wound, then replaced the dressing.

I tilted my head to search your face and saw the fear from earlier that stopped me abruptly. We locked eyes, sharing a nonverbal connection for long moments. I could almost hear the sounds of the guns and the breaking glass vibrating between us.

"Do you want to talk about it?" I finally asked. The silence stretched for so long that I wondered if you'd heard me. After a while you tightened your hold and shifted more securely in my lap. Tears welled in your eyes. "Baby, it's okay," I whispered against your skin.

"He reached for the gun. All I could see was his hand reaching for it. I—I didn't see you..." A single tear tracked down your face. I brushed it away with my thumb. For the first time I realized that you were experiencing the same fear for me. My heart broke watching the raw agony that played across your features. I had no idea what to say because I was just as traumatized by the events. We'd stared down a cop shooter, responded with force and killed a man, risking everything. *Everything.* The memory of your stricken face mirroring my panic drove the danger frighteningly home. The peril of loving another cop made crystal clear.

But we survived. You trembled against me. I wrapped my arms tightly around your neck and buried my face in your hair, drawing comfort from the feel and the scent of you. "It's okay," I whispered. "I'm okay. We both are. Shh..." I threaded my fingers though your dark hair and placed feather-light kisses along your shoulder, up your neck to your face. "I'm here, Mandy." Our lips met softly. You kept your eyes open as if to reassure yourself that it was the truth. Your hazel eyes change color like a mood ring, always allowing me to read your emotions and needs. What I saw was deep indigo, smoldering with desire so intense that I shuddered in anticipation of your touch. I felt heat from your center on my stomach, and your mouth quirked up at the corners with just a trace of a smile. You touched the tip of your tongue to my lips and traced their outline slowly before gently entering to begin the enticing slow dance with mine.

Soon my head was spinning and my breathing ragged. I shifted my pelvis trying to bring you into tighter contact with my torso. You began a slow thrusting motion that left me desperate to feel your heated sex gripping my fingers. With the pad of one finger I traced your contours with light caresses, carefully avoiding the sensitive tip of your clitoris as you moaned softly in my ear. Your hand stole down my abdomen, sliding into my sensitive folds.

Your tongue flicked my stiffened nipple to the same rhythm as your finger at my center. I drove my hands into your thick hair and pulled you more firmly against my breast, forcing it into your mouth. Soon you turned your attention to the other breast, sliding your tongue across the valley between them as you moved, to perform the same ritual, alternately sucking, nipping, devouring while your finger continued to exquisitely torment the base of my clit. My blood roared in my head with the overload of glorious sensation that radiated through every nerve ending of my body. This was life itself. Life we might have lost.

I felt the delicious tingle of my building climax ripple from my stomach toward my center, the pressure intensified with each practiced stroke from you. Coherent thought became impossible as the buzzing in my brain blocked out any other sensations save your incredible touch. Both of us moaned with pleasure. Knowing your body, your need, I slid two fingers smoothly inside and your clit jumped and throbbed against my thumb. You shifted again, forcing my fingers deeper inside. You took my nipple in your mouth, and I felt the vibration of your satisfied chuckle against my breast as your superb torment drew a new gasp from my throat.

I leaned my head back and could hear us driving each other to orgasm through the water. Our arm movements made soft whooshing sounds. The combination of sensations and sounds sent my body soaring toward climax and your pulsing muscles gripped and pulled me more firmly inside. Deeper. Harder. Yes.

You dropped your head to my shoulder as I cradled you in my lap. The physical release gave way to a tenderness that threatened to undo me altogether, and I fought tears that burned my eyes. My hand was still inside you, feeling your tremors slowly fade. You wrapped your arms tightly around me and I surrendered completely into your certain embrace. You painted feather-light kisses along my neck and collarbone until I finally stilled. I raised my head to look into your amazing eyes, now a soft satisfied blue that gently gazed at me, and I was overcome once again by the depth of our love.

You smiled sweetly and placed a delicate kiss on my lips.

Then you whispered, "Welcome home."

ARE YOU MY MOMMY?

Danielle Mignon

I never realized I wanted to be spanked until the day I called my girlfriend "Mom."

Actually, I'd called Louisa "Mom" many times before, but always in my trademark self-reflexive mock-teenager tone. For instance, she might ask me to please eat something healthy for dinner and I might say, "Yes, Mom," or she might comment on what a mess my apartment was and I might say, "I'll clean it tomorrow, Mom." It was conscious and innocuous and always, always a joke.

This "Mom" was different.

In truth, I can't recall what I was so worked up about at the time. Something career-related, most likely. I remember Louisa sitting on the edge of my bed, fully dressed. I was nearly naked and standing between her thighs. My arms rested on her shoulders, my body nestled into the warm comfort of her cleavage as I whined about whatever the trouble was. She ran her hands through my hair in consolation and suddenly I said, "I don't know what to do about it, Mom."

I didn't hear it until after I'd said it, and by that time, of course, I couldn't take it back. My spine straightened, vertebra by vertebra, until I was standing straight as an arrow.

"Did you hear that?" I asked. "I just called you Mom."

Louisa didn't react at all the way I expected. She just laughed and said, "Freud would have a field day."

"You're not..." Not what? Angry? Upset? Afraid? I didn't even know what I was asking. "I mean, that's weird. Right? Calling my girlfriend Mom?"

"Do you love me?"

"Yes."

She held my hands, swinging them out to the sides. "And you love your mother?"

"Of course I do."

"And your mother and I are basically the same age?"

I hesitated, which was stupid because it was a rhetorical question. Louisa knew very well she was nearly as old as my mother. Hell, she had more in common with my mom than she had with me. Sometimes I thought if we ever broke up... Well, that was silly. Louisa would be mine forever.

"You're not mad?" I asked, feeling beyond juvenile. That was such a childish question, but I couldn't think of a better one in the moment.

She ran her hands over the curve of my ass, squeezing. "Why would I be mad?"

Luckily, Louisa had always been one of those super-mature partners who didn't mind listening to stories about other lovers. So I said, "My ex would have freaked out."

Her blue eyes sparkled like aquamarines, and the knowing smile on her lips told me she understood. Even so, she cocked her head and asked, "Why?"

"Because of the age difference." I ran my fingers across Louisa's lips until she nipped at me and I pulled away, laughing. "She was a year older than you, and she always worried people would think I was her daughter."

I took a chance then, leaning in to kiss my girl. She didn't nip at me this time. She returned my kiss, slow and sensual, our tongues mingling like two sizzling serpents. That day I had on my black velvet camisole, the one with the black lace across the top, and Louisa took hold of the straps, pulling them down my arms until the stretchy fabric rested around my hips.

"Why did she care?" Louisa asked as I crawled into her lap, straddling her broad thighs.

"Hmm?"

"Your ex." She cupped my naked breasts. The warmth of her palms on my not-yet-hard nipples made me moan. "Why did she care so much what other people thought?"

"Oh, it wasn't just other people." Normally I wouldn't have been keen on discussing old relationships in bed with my new girlfriend, but there was something about Louisa that just opened me up. I wanted to reveal myself, in all my imperfect glory. "It's like she was afraid of what we thought of ourselves, or afraid of all the hidden stuff inside our heads. If you think I'm Jungian, she was, like, ultra-Jungian with a hint of Freudian guilt in there somewhere."

Louisa looked me in the eye while her hands pulsed against my breasts, and I knew she had no idea what I was talking about.

I tried again. "There were things she wouldn't do because they played too much into the age dynamic. Anything that came close to age play was totally out of bounds. If I'd called her Mommy in the bedroom she would have been upset. If I'd slipped like I did just now and called her Mom by accident? Jesus, I think her head would have exploded. She would have run a mile."

"See, I don't get that." Louisa let out a little growl as she pinched my nipples, then rolled them between her fingers and thumbs until I squealed. "Everybody brings a parent/child dynamic to romantic relationships. Even if we were the same age, that dynamic would be there to a certain extent, it's just accentuated with us because I'm older and you're younger."

"I know," I said, hissing gently. She still hadn't let go of my tits. "I agree with you, but my ex was ridiculously afraid I wanted her to be my mother, or that I saw her that way, or... well, whatever."

"And did you?" Louisa asked idly, like the question was insignificant.

Something inside me froze while my body jerked forward. Before I knew what I was doing, I'd shoved my tits in Louisa's face, rubbing my pebbled little nipples against her lips. God, that felt good, the way they sort of stuck to her tacky lipstick, picking up traces of the stuff. Soon enough my tits had gone from subtle pink to shimmering reddish-brown.

"Aren't you going to suck my tits?" I took her head in my hands, tempting her with one breast and then the other.

"Is that what you want?" She smiled that impish smile I knew so well.

"Yes."

I didn't think she'd do it, at least not right away. I thought she'd tease me a little longer, running her lips side to side across my tits, maybe licking them with that hot velvet tongue. But I was wrong. Louisa wrapped her mouth around my breast, over-shooting my nipple and sucking half my little boob into her big bad mouth.

"Oh, baby!" When she bit my pursed nipple, I wrapped my hands around her head and moaned. "God, you're good at this."

She switched sides, glancing up at me before taking my other tit in her mouth. "So, what would your ex have done if you'd asked for a spanking?"

I laughed, because never in a million years would she have gone for that. "She probably would have explained to me, very calmly, that spanking would feel too much like a mother disciplining her daughter and she wasn't interested in exploring that realm of our relationship."

"What about you?" Louisa's mouth hovered over my nipple, and her warm breath made my pussy ache. "Were you interested in exploring that realm of your relationship?"

"Hmm?" I found it hard to focus with her mouth so close to my breast. "With her? Not really. We had good sex, so I was happy."

I nudged my tit at her lips, but she turned her face up to look at me. "What about with us? How would you like it if I spanked you?"

My pussy clamped down on nothing and my heart beat fast. "You would do that?"

Louisa shrugged, suddenly indifferent, though I knew it was an act. "If that's what you wanted, sure."

"I want you to suck my tits," I said, forcing my breast against her mouth until she opened up at last. When she wrapped those perfect lips around my nipple, my pussy begged for attention. "Oh God, baby, can you finger-fuck me too?"

"You sure do ask for a lot," she mumbled without drawing completely away from my breast.

"That's because you're so good at everything."

My blatant flattery worked. Louisa snuck one hand between my thighs. She felt around, tracing her soft fingers up and down my slit before entering me from behind. I arched forward, shoving my breast into her mouth as she fucked me. One finger at first, then two. Three of her large fingers were really all I could bear in my tight little cunt, and when she pumped them inside me I bucked back against them, wanting more, always more.

Even though she'd just asked me if I wanted a spanking, I admit I wasn't ready when her heavy hand fell against my ass. I gasped, straightening up, looking her plain in the eye. She was smiling, of course.

"You didn't like that?" she asked.

"I...did." I couldn't move. Thank goodness Louisa had a grip on my waist to keep me from toppling over. "That was my first spanking, you know."

"I know." She spanked me again. "And that was your second."

At first I wasn't clear on which hand she'd used to spank me, but when I felt my pussy juice slathered across my ass and realized her fingers were no longer inside me, I knew it must be the hand she'd finger-fucked me with.

I let myself go and tumbled against Louisa, hooking my chin over her shoulder. She was so steady, so reliable. When Louisa was around, I knew I was safe.

Her hand struck my ass again, and this third spanking was the first I remember actually feeling. The first two were novelty, pure fun, but this one slammed my skin unforgivingly, making me wince.

"Oh god, Louisa." I kissed her neck, sucking skin that tasted faintly of pressed powder and salt. "That was amazing."

"What, this?" She spanked me again, same spot, and a dull burn began. When I closed my eyes, I could see her red hand-print on my ass. She'd left her mark on me. And again, another clout. "You like this?"

"God, yes." I bit her shoulder as she brought her hot palm

down on my ass once again, keeping it there when the blow was struck. I couldn't believe how blazing my skin was, or how hard she was smacking me. "Fuck, that feels so good."

"You like getting spanked?" She rubbed both her palms around both my cheeks, teasing me before slapping my ass with two hands. "You like getting spanked by Mommy?"

My stomach flipped. It sounded weird. It sounded so weird that I didn't know how to respond.

"No?" she asked.

"I..." What could I say? I wanted her to keep going. "I like it. A lot."

"Oh you do?" She smacked my ass again, the right cheek, then the left, right, left, alternating until it burned so badly I reached behind to shield myself from the blows.

"If you like it, why are you blocking your ass?"

"It hurts," I said, thinking that would be enough to stop her.

No chance. Louisa pulled my hands away and spanked my ass again. "I thought you liked getting spanked by Mommy."

"By you!" I cried, trying to cover my ass. "Not by Mommy, by you!"

"By me?" she asked, sounding all sweet and innocent as she ripped my hands away from my bum. "You want to be spanked by me?"

She didn't wait for an answer. Louisa walloped my blazing ass. One spanking, two, three, four. I lost count because my head wouldn't stop buzzing. "Oh god, it hurts. Baby, it hurts. It hurts so bad."

"And you like it?"

Tears pricked my eyes. I felt hot all over. "Yes!"

"And you want more?"

I struggled and writhed against her, but I couldn't escape her grip. "I want more!"

Louisa spanked me and I arched against her frame as if she would protect me from herself. "You like it, don't you?"

"It hurts!" I hollered, releasing the tears that had welled in my eyes. They streamed down my cheeks as I screamed with the pain of every new blow.

I squirmed like a rabbit trying to escape a child's grip, but it was no use. Louisa held me firmly in place as she whacked my tender ass. My skin was so red and hot and hurting it almost felt like it wasn't part of my body anymore.

"If you've had enough, just say *enough* and I'll stop." Louisa struck me yet again, and I wanted to say it but I couldn't. It was the strangest feeling, wanting more and wanting it to end. Every spanking was torture now. I was crying, actually crying, and still I couldn't ask her to stop.

Suddenly we were on the move, and I clung to Louisa's shoulders because I thought I was falling. No, not falling...sliding? Louisa pulled me up on the bed and shifted until she was lying on her back and I was snuggled into her front.

The spankings seemed to have stopped, but still I felt on edge. They'd begun so abruptly and continued so forcefully that I couldn't be sure those pretty palms of hers had finished their work.

After a few long breaths, Louisa bent to my ear and whispered, "I think you've had enough."

A smile of relief bled across my lips as my body melted into hers. "Oh, thank god! That hurt like a bitch, but I couldn't ask you to stop."

"You couldn't ask your mommy to stop or you couldn't ask your girlfriend to stop?"

I smirked against her shoulder, closing my eyes. My cheeks were still wet with tears, and my ass burned like the fires of hell. I was naked and sweating and aroused and satisfied all at once.

"You're not going to answer that question, are you?" Louisa teased.

She knew me too well. "Of course not."

LOST BATTERIES

Jasmine Grimstead

Leslie's body haunted me.

Our mutual friends were all hedonists. While I sat on the couch drinking Merlot in college during parties, Taylor and Wright and their entourage would be in the back room flirting with substances I was sure probably weren't legal, all to spill out of the room together naked and dancing. Leslie would be with them, her wild curls bouncing with her breasts as she'd shimmy her way back into the crowd, propelling herself from one set of arms to another. I wasn't out yet and I was always terrified someone that hadn't been in the back room would notice my eyes on Leslie's pale skin, on her mahogany bush.

The parties weren't the only times I'd have to peel my eyes away from her. When it got too hot in the summer and our friends were restless, we'd pack into a station wagon and head for the local watering hole everyone called Snake Pit. No one ever brought a bathing suit. I was always careful to keep my body from the neck down underwater. The boys thought it was because I was too shy to let them see much of me, but it was always because I was hiding erect nipples from being turned on by Leslie's body stretched out sunning on a rock. The day she asked me to spread aloe on her burnt shoulders when we were packing up our wet towels, I excused myself from the task by saying I needed to go check my body for leeches. I was terrified that I'd give myself away if I touched her.

The universe, it seemed, was always trying to tease me. While she was unquestionably comfortable in her skin, I had never seen her do anything with anyone, even when some of the parties we had been to together had escalated into near orgies. Whether shaving her legs the morning after a party in the bathroom at our friends' house with the door hanging open, or eating a nectarine at lunch, she was always sensual. I just didn't know if she was actively sexual, despite the fact that I had noticed that I wasn't the only one who seemed to want her.

None of the guys ever seemed to have any kind of effect on her. Less surprisingly, I felt like I didn't show up on her radar at all. We went on the same adventures and outings together more often than not, but we shared friends and space more than we shared a connection. I was always on the periphery and she was out of reach.

The night of the first meteor shower of our junior year of college, we decided to find a patch of woods up in the mountains with just enough clearing to see the stars from and throw a party. We filled picnic baskets with strawberries, cheap wine, and chocolates, and spread out our blankets so we could lie on our backs and watch the sky once it was late enough for something to start happening. A battery-powered stereo rescued from someone's mother's attic played music for us in the event that anyone felt like dancing. Overall, it had a nice effect, but

I was fairly sure that everyone's clothing was going to stay on. That was disappointing.

After the setting up was over and it was dark enough for people to start showing, Leslie made her way over to me.

"Brianna, I think I dropped some of the stereo batteries from my bag on the way from the car and I want to find them in case the ones we're using now don't last the night. Since it's getting dark, I was wondering if you could come with me?"

Taylor's ears seemed to have tuned in from across the clearing. "If Brianna doesn't want to go along, I'd be happy to go with you!"

"Don't worry about it, Taylor," I said quickly. "I have a flashlight, so I'll go with her." I grabbed it from my back pocket, flicked it on and turned to start walking into the woods so that he couldn't push it any further. I smiled at Leslie, walking beside me.

"Thank you—Taylor's been a little too persistent lately. Besides, I feel like you never really spend any time with me." While I didn't meet her gaze, I felt her eyes on me. I couldn't explain that I avoided her like the plague because I desperately wanted to bite down on her sides where they curved and her skin would be sensitive. Or that I wanted to swim underwater and see if her bottom half had turned into a mermaid tail every time we went to the lake together.

"Happy to be of service," I said. "Where do you think you lost them?"

"A bit further in," she said, motioning with her light. "Up there somewhere."

I nodded and tried to think of something to say. It was hard to breathe beside her, and I was afraid she would think the short distance we had already walked had me winded already. Leslie was athletic and had a feminine but toned body from all the running and yoga she was always doing. While I didn't want her to know I wanted her, having her think I was totally out of shape would somehow be equally embarrassing.

Her stride was strong and fast, too quiet except for the crunching of the leaves below us until she broke the silence. "Are you wishing for anything tonight?" she asked.

"Not for anything that I'd trust the shooting stars to give me. What about you?"

She stopped beside me. I swore I could feel a hush settling around us. I felt something coming—a tingle shooting down my spine that I normally only got when incense was lit or when I was right in front of the stage at a concert and could feel a strong bass vibration shooting up my leg.

"I've always wanted to kiss you," she said, "but I thought instead of wishing, I'd just make it happen." She flicked her flashlight off and threw it on the ground, and then reached for mine and did the same while I tried to process. She stepped forward and cupped my face in her tiny hands, and brought her mouth to mine in a way that made all the slow-motion scenes in movies I'd never understood before make sense.

I tasted the cinnamon of her clove cigarettes mixed with the hemp balm she wore on her lips and felt my body begin to react now that contact had become a reality. My hands were already in the tangles and waves of her hair, windblown from riding with the windows down earlier. She caught my tongue in her mouth and sucked on it, then moved her hands back to my face to keep my mouth still as she licked the outside of my lips before diving in to kiss me more deeply. As we kissed, Leslie pushed me backward and we stumbled together, unwilling to let go, until my back hit the nearest tree. When I'd come up for oxygen, I kissed my way up her jaw. I nuzzled her long, swanlike neck with my cheek and whispered into her ear, "My wish is that you don't stop."

She looked at me meaningfully as if for confirmation and then dove in when she saw she had it. Her hands were underneath my shirt, steadily rising toward my breasts in their thin lace bra. She cupped my breasts and then pushed them up, aggressive, sending my back to meet the tree behind me again. She kneaded them—a rough massage that showed she wasn't afraid to touch me the way I was so terrified of touching her. My entire body, from my posture to my mental state, was in direct submission.

"We don't have much time." She peeled her own clothing off in fluid motions, breasts bare beneath her tunic, tiny black cotton boy shorts covering the sinful curve of her ass. My clothes were on the forest floor in no time but my excitement was equally matched with my fear. I had absolutely no idea what to do with a woman outside of kissing her.

Leslie eased me down onto the forest floor so that I was flat on my back, skin sensitive to the wet grass and rocks below me. She kissed her way down my body from the hollow of my throat to the band of my lace thong, stopping to give each breast a thorough examination with her expert mouth. She pushed both of my breasts together, hard, to the point where bruises would emerge later to mark where her fingertips had been. She buried her face between them, nuzzling me with her soft skin before licking each nipple in slow, wet, drawn-out circles. When I moaned, I could feel her lips curve to smile above me before she went in for the kill, sucking and biting. The cold metal from her tongue piercing mixed with the wetness of her mouth sent shivers down my spine that I couldn't stifle. The pleasure made me forget the edges of rock and sticks digging into my shoulders and ass.

As she trailed downward, away from my breasts, her long hair moved over my body and caressed my skin where her hands didn't. In her hair I could smell the scents of the apple butter and the fried food in the restaurant she cooked at down the mountain for extra money. She smelled like a mountain woman—like comfort and the food she'd bring from work to all of the parties we'd go to.

She bit down on the space where my skin ended and my thong started, grabbing the fabric between her teeth. She moved her mouth downward, removing my panties with just her teeth and a little extra help from me. Once I was bare, she removed her own panties and mounted me, bringing her face down close to mine.

As she began to move back and forth over me, her sex over mine, her breathing changed. I reached down to my pussy and pulled the skin above it back so that my clit was better exposed, and leaned back so that she could grind hers into it. We locked into a steady rhythm, my body bucking below hers, her natural curls against my smooth, shaved skin. Her hands clamped down again on my breasts as she fell back over me, using her grip to steady herself as she ground circles into my body.

She was a sexy wood nymph, and I felt barely real myself, reduced to a heap of buzzing atoms. I sent a pagan prayer up to thank the gods for battery-powered stereos, and for my sexual tension not being one-sided. The way the stars were shining above Leslie's back as she gyrated made me sure that they heard me.

"I was afraid you wouldn't want this," she said devilishly into the sweat at the side of my face, "but you want it as much as I do. You know how I know?"

I shook my head, unable to speak. All my concentration was taken up by my nerve endings. There wasn't any left over for trying to communicate, so I licked my lips and fluttered my eyes up at her, waiting for her to tell me.

Leslie lifted herself off me and lay down, moving her hand to my pussy and stroking it idly before inserting a finger inside so that it darted in and out of just the entrance, a gentle tease. When she removed her finger, she brought it up to my mouth. I closed my lips down over her finger and moved them up and down, sucking as I tasted myself on her skin.

"I know because of how wet you are for me."

"If you think this is bad," I said, taking her hand from my mouth and holding it in both of mine, kissing and nibbling it in between my words, "you should have felt me the first time I saw you dancing naked at Taylor's house. I'm more interested in tasting you, though, than tasting me."

Confident and ready to give me what I'd asked for, she mounted me again, this time with her knees at either side of my head on the ground. She leaned forward, hugging the base of the tree she'd pushed me into earlier for support.

I bit into the flesh of her legs, varying the degree of pressure with each nibble, making my way back and forth between each thigh and working up higher every time my teeth hit her skin. As I did so, my hands worked her ass, pulling her down closer to my mouth so that her knees slid out further. Enveloped in her damp smell, I wanted to taste her more than I'd ever wanted whiskey or steak or wine.

I used my hands to part her sex. The first lick was slow from front to back, letting me collect each bit of moisture on my tongue as I reveled in her, trying to show restraint and be slow and sensual before I ravished her. I moved my tongue in and out of her pussy and she ground herself into me, frantic, making low whimpering noises.

It wasn't long before I knew she was on the brink, her legs shaking, one of her hands knotting in my hair while her other arm was still desperately clinging to the tree, her face pressed against it. I used my tongue in her pussy along with two fingers and worked them in and out, covering them in moisture, and then used them to rub her juices onto her clit before going back to town inside her. With her pussy packed full, I used my free hand to spread her lips again so that I had plenty of space around her clit for my tongue to dance across every nerve ending while I sucked off her nectar.

Everything felt right, there in the woods, her body and our sex such a natural extension of our surroundings that I marveled at the fact that the idea hadn't been mine first. A woman as free as Leslie didn't belong on a bed trapped between rumpled sheets, but out under the open sky where she could be as wild as she wanted to, dirt below her knees and her sweat running into the fallen summer leaves.

The closer she got, the slower my licks became, to build the volume of her orgasm instead of delivering it more quickly. When she tried to increase the speed by wiggling her ass and cunt so she could control how fast it was coming, I stopped licking altogether until she realized that she had to let me be in charge of the delivery. Once I resumed my licking, her muscle spasms came in short spurts, her clit jumping from my tongue as the contractions stopped and started again, a long growl escaping from her lips. Liquid sweetness ran down onto my face from the fleshy rose tissue inside her once her body finally stilled, and I licked it away with the same reverence I gave to the last morsel of a gourmet meal on the rare occasion I was afforded one. Leslie's taste was a delicacy.

She dismounted and tumbled back onto the ground beside me, her face flushed and glowing through the darkness. She draped one of her arms across me and pulled me closer.

I stroked her hair while she recovered. "If we don't get back, they'll think we've gone missing."

"We can only go back now on one condition," she said, perching on her elbow and looking down at me.

"What's that?"

"That if we go back now, after the meteor shower you let my fingers go missing inside you."

Her fingers went missing inside my pussy multiple times that night and nearly every night after. The next time Leslie and I hunted down batteries, it was in a sex toy store, and they were for our vibrator.

ODDS

Catherine Henreid

I sink against the wall. At last the tears start to fall. My damp hair falls into my face and I feel how chilly the air is and how clammy the wall is. I sit down on the floor in a small corner that's still dry and hide my face in my hands. The last hour passes before my eyes. I can't believe the bad luck it brought.

About an hour ago, I was getting ready to go to a Shabbat dinner my friend Britta is throwing. There's not much to do on a Friday evening in Israel, even in Tel Aviv. Most places close by the late afternoon, forcing everyone, Jewish or not, to power down and unwind. That includes us, overseas students from all around the world. We party Thursday night and Saturday night and many of the nights in between, but Friday is our lazy day. Nevertheless, I was excited to go. Britta is a great cook and everyone brings something, turning dinners at her house into a student version of fusion cuisine from at least half a dozen countries. I'd made sweet potato soup. The warm smell of the spices still filled our small apartment, but now it mingled with the scent of my perfume.

Felicity, my roommate, glanced at me applying lip gloss in front of the mirror outside the bathroom. "Going to Britta's?"

"Yeah." I nodded. "You coming?"

"Nah. I'm chilling. Maybe meeting the guys at Danny's place later. Looking good," she called over her shoulder before disappearing into the kitchen. I heard her turning on the microwave.

"Don't take the soup!" I called after her, but didn't get an answer. I knew she was rolling her eyes at me. She often does.

We have different views of how living together is supposed to be. Or what an apartment should look like. We don't argue over whose turn it is to do the dishes. We sorted that out at the very beginning, and it has been working pretty well so far. It's more basic stuff. We're going to be here for another sixteen months. It's important to me that we make this place feel like a home as best we can. I don't get how she doesn't see what a dump it is—or why she doesn't mind.

The apartment has its good sides, no doubt. A huge balcony. A fully furnished kitchen. Almost no cockroaches. I've definitely seen worse—like the university dorms. That's why I started looking for an apartment. I couldn't afford to live on my own, so I searched for a roommate among the other students in the program.

And the place looks much nicer now than it did when we moved in. I bought a tablecloth to cover the kitchen table, which looked as if it'd been in use for generations. I decorated the balcony with plants and cushions. I put the angel-shaped candle my mom gave me as a parting gift on the fridge. And I ordered copies of photos of us and our friends from the program, pictures I took at parties, school trips, or at the beach. I had them enlarged and taped them over the cracks in the walls, especially on the narrow walls of the crooked corridor between our rooms. It's the darkest part of the apartment, because there's no window, no lamp and the ceiling is suspended. The only light comes from the adjacent bathroom, if we keep its door opened.

Felicity never commented on any of my efforts at embellishment.

So this rare occasion of being complimented by her was music to my ears. Not that I'm looking for her approval. I don't try to dress up for her or anything. I simply like looking pretty. It's something that's important to me.

She couldn't care less. Felicity's idea of dressing up is to don a shirt instead of a tee and to change into fresh jeans.

She's not a bad person. Maybe just not the ideal roommate. Sometimes, though, we sit on her shabby couch—I never asked where she got it, because I'm afraid of the answer, but at least she put a blanket over it—and we watch a movie together after I've prepared something for dinner. It feels cozy. I'm not really sure why, since her room lacks the things that usually make a room feel homey.

I thought back to when I first met her. It was in the early days of the program and there were so many new faces and exotic accents that I was happy just to remember the names of the people from my Hebrew class. She was one of the students who had answered my ad on the university's blackboard. I had just closed the door behind a guy from the Netherlands when the doorbell rang again. Outside in the hallway stood a pale, skinny girl with an unruly pixie haircut. Her upper lip had a defiant curve.

While I was still trying to decide what it was that made her oddly attractive, she held out her hand to me. "Felicity."

I let her in and checked her out more closely. The baggy

jeans. The broad leather belt. The unbuttoned shirt. The wife-beater underneath. The plain silver bracelet. And the tattoo on her wrist. Felicity?

She looked at me and grinned. "What name would you prefer? Shane?"

I blushed. How did she...?

She nodded toward a half-unpacked suitcase and I followed her gaze. On top was my DVD case, lying open. "You know *The L-Word*?" I asked, a bit incredulous.

"Sure," she said, as if I had asked her if she wanted a glass of water. I led her into the kitchen and offered her something to drink. She took a look around the room. "Felicity's my grand-ma's name, okay?"

"I... I'm sorry. I didn't mean to—"

"Yes, you did." There was a little twinkle in her eyes, and I knew she wasn't offended. I couldn't be offended either. Although it was kind of rude, wasn't it? Looking back, I know she was just being candid.

Anyway, she seemed to be the most genuine of all the people who came to look at the place, so I asked her to move in with me. She gave me a broad smile, and the next day, there she was, with a suitcase and a backpack. I was a bit shocked that that was all the luggage she had, but she just shrugged. In the weeks following, she collected the little furniture that she deemed necessary to make a home. Basically, it's just a bed and the moth-eaten couch. A chair and dresser already were in the room.

These past few months have been a blast. I've never felt more alive than I have since I came here. If the city has a hymn, it must be "Shiny Happy People." Everybody's always flirting and playing and dancing. And I don't mean only us, the foreigners, overwhelmed by the city's smells and its shabby beauty and the sparkling of its thousands of lights in the sea at night. Maybe it's the atrocities these people have seen that make them want to party hard and live life to the fullest.

Tel Aviv is full of beautiful women. Beautiful men too. I don't know if it's the sunshine that makes everyone's skin tanned and hair glossy and eyes shining, or the many different corners of the world that come together in this city and its people, or simply the vanity of the place.

Felicity doesn't differentiate, not between races, not between nationalities and not between sexes. She once told me she thinks when you long for someone, you long for the person, not the gender. I think that was the most vulnerable she has ever allowed herself to be in front of me.

I like things to be a bit more organized. For me at least. It confuses me when I meet a guy in our kitchen one morning and then she brings home some chick the next week. I don't mind the boys. Most of them are very polite. Sometimes they are so nice that I feel sorry for them and I make them break-fast because I know they will never come back. I can see in the eyes of some that they hope they will, but in the end, Felicity never lets them. They always thank me. Felicity rarely acts as if she cares. It irritates me. And the girls irritate me. They are all the same type. High-maintenance. Long tresses, doe eyes, and petite. Their skin is smooth and golden. And they look at me as if I were the competition. They never come back either, so I let them. But I never offer them so much as a cup of coffee.

I slipped into my jacket and left my room the moment she came out of the kitchen. "Okay. Have fun!" I said, grabbing my keys.

She mumbled something like "You too."

I hesitated for a moment, contemplating whether to take a scarf with me. It's early February, and it's getting cold at night, even in the Mediterranean.

Suddenly, there was a bang, followed by a short rumble. Our eyes turned to the direction of the noise, the bathroom corridor, but everything remained quiet. I ran back into my room to get the scarf, and when I returned, Felicity had already gone back into hers. She turned up the music, but I still heard it.

The sound of water dripping on stone.

I narrowed my eyes and saw a line running down the pale yellowish wall, darker than the rest. It wasn't much, just a thin trickle. While my mind tried to get around the fact that water was appearing out of nowhere on our ceiling, the trickle became a stream. I put down my bag, rushed into the bathroom and grabbed the cleaning bucket and a towel.

"Felicity! Felicity, there's a leak somewhere above." She didn't hear me. I was peeved. I wanted to get going. I ran into the kitchen and gathered pots and bowls. "Felicity!" I yelled and patted the wall with the towel. It was soaked within moments, and still the water kept running down the wall. "Felicity!"

"What?!" Her head appeared in the door.

I pointed to the water that, by then, was already running down both walls and splattering with heavy drops into the accumulation of pots and bowls on the ground. She simply stared. I rolled my eyes, brushed past her and grabbed all the towels I could find. I threw them at the growing puddle, but I might as well have tried to quell a fire with a glass of water. The dark patches on the wall got bigger.

"Get your towels, bedsheets—whatever!" I snarled at her.

She finally started to move, and a few moments later returned, her arms full of linens. I grabbed some and pressed them against the edge where the wall meets the ceiling. Hot water ran down my arm. Felicity kneeled down, collected the towels I'd tossed on the floor and wrung them out over the bathtub.

I cursed as the leak grew bigger, and I was about to tell her to come and help me when there was a hissing sound, another crack, not so heavy this time, and torrents of hot water poured down on me. I was soaked within seconds, and too shocked to even shriek.

I brushed the masses of wet hair out of my face, and when the steam had cleared, I saw Felicity in the bathroom door, not entirely unaffected by the flood from above, albeit not as dripping as I was. Her mouth twitched.

"It's not funny!" I felt like crying, but I didn't. Instead, I stepped aside, peeled myself out of the jacket and shot a furious glance at her. I didn't get to give her a piece of my mind because the water, sloshing toward the entrance of my room, took all of my attention. I jumped toward the door, splashing more water at Felicity as I passed her and slammed it shut. I took whatever was left of the towels and rolled them up against the door, then ran over to Felicity's room and did the same. Felicity emptied the bucket and the pots over the bathtub, but they were filled again so quickly that most of it slopped out and onto the floor. For a while, we worked in silence, but I already knew it was in vain. The water stood fingers deep in our entrance area, and out of the corner of my eye, I could see the towels, meant to keep it from running into my room, were completely soaked. Feeling desperate, I mopped the water toward the bathroom.

Eventually, when the immediate danger was turned away from our rooms, Felicity straightened up and vanished around the corner. She came back into the corridor with her cell phone in hand and mouthed "landlord." I continued swabbing the floor and heard her apologizing for disturbing him on Shabbat eve, then briefly describing our situation. She said "yes" a few times, and that she understood, before flipping the phone shut. "He's not coming."

The water on my skin had grown cold. My clothes clung

to my body. I got up, realizing we were alone with this. "You should have made him. You should have insisted! After all—"

A puff interrupted my rant, and the lights went out. The fridge gave a hollow shudder and became silent. The droning buzz from the air conditioner died down.

I sniffed. "What do we do? Felicity, what should we do?"

"I don't know!" She sounded annoyed, and somehow more with me than with our situation.

I didn't care. The horror of the night that lay ahead crept up in my belly and began to consume me. No electricity, no heating, no hot water. Until Sunday. I got up and wiped my eyes. If something like this has to happen, it had better not happen on a Shabbat eve in Israel.

"There's got to be something," I whined.

Felicity looked at the mess around us and shrugged.

"If you don't care, I—" I started, but she pinned me against the wall.

"Shut up! Shut the fuck up!" She lifted her hand and for a moment, I was certain she'd slap me.

She didn't slap me. Instead, she kissed me. Hard and fierce and more for herself than for me. It was a kiss to shut me up. Her body pressed into mine, and for a short moment, there was warmth. There was cover. Then she turned on her heels and rushed out of the apartment.

The door slammed into the latch and numb, shivering, I watched my photographs curling up and sliding down the walls, into the puddle that was our hallway.

I cry a bit more. Felicity's probably already over at Danny's, and he'll give her a pair of his pants to wear—not much difference there anyway—and they'll have a beer and a laugh while Felicity regales the guys with the story of a little girl standing in the middle of the hallway, dripping from her hair down to her toes. I furiously wipe my cheeks and stare into the twilight that is falling over the apartment.

That's when I see the switch for the boiler, which provides the warm water for our bathroom. It's pointing down. One of us must have forgotten to turn it off. The landlord had told us not to keep it on for too long, but he never said why.

My fury at Felicity flares up again, but it might have been me. Actually... I'm the only one who took a shower this afternoon. Shame shoots into my cheeks. I quickly turn my mind away from the pattern of thoughts that leads to the only possible conclusion: It's my fault that I'm sitting here, soaked, freezing, miserable. I'm the one who ruined our apartment.

I wish I knew why she kissed me. I wonder if she will mention the kiss when she returns?

The music, some bluesy rock tunes, still comes from Felicity's room, but I know that'll be gone too, as soon as the laptop's batteries run out of power. I dread that moment. Her favorite music in the background at least gives me the illusion I'm not alone. I wish I could warm up my soup. Every option I act out in my head to feel less pitiful—blow-dry my hair, make myself some coffee, take a hot shower, snuggle between the covers and watch a movie, drive over to Britta's—eventually falls flat. It's the first time since I arrived in Israel that I miss home.

My heart skips a beat when I hear the rattling of keys, something clonking against the doorknob, a hissing sound, a curse, and then Felicity's tattered jeans appear before my eyes. She bends down. The smell of mint tea fills my nose. She's holding out two cups and as soon as I take one, she yanks her finger to her lips and sucks at it. While I follow her every move like an idiot, she puts the thermos bottle she'd been carrying under her arm on the floor.

I imbibe the tea's pungent, fresh aroma. It's too hot to drink, but just to close my fingers around the steamy cup and to realize she came back for me is all the comfort I need right now. "Where did you get these?" I hear my own voice, choked up and strangled, and clear my throat.

"There's a guy from Egypt living upstairs," Felicity says and perches down next to me. "He said these things can happen when the boiler's pressure gets too high. And that's where it's hidden..."

We both look at the suspended ceiling.

"I know," I say remorsefully. I avert my eyes and wait for her to point out that I took a shower a good three hours ago, but she remains silent. "Thank you," I croak.

She clinks her cup to mine and we drink the tea in silence. I follow the first sip as it fills my mouth with its honeyed flavor, runs down my throat and seeps through my system. I can't believe she's sitting here next to me, just like that. I can't believe how happy I am all of a sudden. I clutch the cup a bit tighter, but eventually it grows cold between my hands.

"You want some more?" Felicity asks, waving the bottle.

I shake my head. "Maybe later."

She rubs my knee, then jumps up. "Come on. Let's get you into some dry clothes."

I follow her into her room where she hands me a sweater. It's cotton, but it feels stiff. I smile a little. "You know, if you used fabric sof—" I stop myself. "Never mind."

I slip out of my pants, and she watches me. Even though it's already dark by now, I'm still glad I'm wearing lacy black panties. Our eyes meet for a moment as I tug at the hem of my top, and Felicity turns away. I slip into her sweater, and when my head appears again, it's hit by a roll of socks. I sit down on her sofa and slip the cool, dry socks over my feet. My skin is still cold, but I'm beginning to feel as if I'm at a pajama party. Or home on a Saturday night, ready to snuggle in front of the TV.

A faint ring from the hallway yanks me out of my reverie. Britta. I wrinkle my nose. I don't want to tiptoe over the cold, slippery floor. I want to stay on this very spot on Felicity's shabby couch. It's just getting warm. Felicity hands me her phone. I call Britta and tell her about our mishap.

"Are you okay?" she asks as I finish.

I fiddle with the sleeves of Felicity's sweater. "Yeah. Yeah, I'm fine."

"Come over. Stay at my place for the night!"

I think about it for a moment. My hair's still wet, my only winter jacket is soaked and we used up all the towels to seal the doors to our rooms. "I think if I spend even a minute on a bike, I'll catch pneumonia. But thank you!"

"Do you want me to bring you anything?"

"No, you have guests..." I hear Felicity puttering about the kitchen. "We got it." A fuzzy glow fills my belly. For the first time, "we" actually feels like "we."

"But you call me if there's anything I can do."

"I will. Thanks!" I put the phone away and look up as Felicity returns with a candle. My candle, actually. The angel-shaped one. "But that's—"

She silences me with a look. "I bet your mom gave it to you for exactly this purpose."

I have to laugh. Maybe she did. Felicity puts the candle on the chair standing close to her bed. I watch her changing into sweatpants. She's wearing plain boy shorts. Of course she is.

"Awan, the guy from upstairs... He offered to let us stay at his apartment if we'd like."

I take a look around. "Actually, I like it here." I'm surprised at myself that I said that, and even though it makes me feel good, it also makes me nervous. We have no one else to call. Nothing to wait for. Nothing to do. I wrap my arms around my body and rock lightly back and forth on the sofa. She sits down beside me and puts her arm around me.

"I'm sorry, okay? I'm sorry that I yelled at you and...that I kissed you."

My bottom lip disappears beneath my upper one. I'm more disappointed than feels right, given that she's my roommate and I had never wanted her to kiss me and the kiss was so rough and... Why is she grinning at me?

"Actually, I'm not," she says.

Heat shoots into my stomach. "You're not...?"

"Sorry that I kissed you," she says earnestly. She looks at me for a moment, then smoothes my hair out of my face. Oh, this is better than the tea. Sweeter. Intensely soothing. And...electrifying. She withdraws her hand, and the mischief comes back into her features. "I've never kissed a Polonia before."

The butterflies that had just started to twirl in my belly vanish with a pang. While part of me realizes she might just be resorting to humor, a much bigger part of me is indignant. I know that term by now. It's the Israeli way of saying someone acts like a Jewish mother.

I turn my head away and raise my chin. "Well. Of course you've never kissed someone who's caring and— "

"Smothering..." She raises her brow comically.

"Caring," I repeat firmly, "and idealistic and a good cook... You only date JAPs!" Ha.

She laughs. "Jewish American Princesses are cute."

I grumble. My hands play with some loose fringes on the blanket covering the couch. Suddenly I realize how hideous I must look. Mascara smeared all over my cheeks. Hair disheveled and lank. Thighs completely unprotected by flattering clothes.

Felicity takes my hand. "I like living with you, okay? I don't care for the tablecloth or the flower pots or the French toast, but it's nice to have you around."

It's as if her clothes empower me. Or her smell lingering in the rough material makes me bold. This time, I kiss her.

If she's surprised, she gets over it quickly. Her mouth opens warmly against mine. I can taste the mint on her lips and the honey on her tongue. She pulls me onto her lap and cups my butt. She squeezes it a bit and groans. I pull her closer to me; I can't help but smile at her reaction to my body in her arms. Her fingers wander underneath the sweater. She strokes the small of my back and runs her fingertips up my spine. My skin reacts immediately. I straighten up, just like the soft hairs do in the wake of her touch. I shudder and kiss her more fiercely.

Her hands tickle my sides as she moves them to pull down the cups of my bra, and my groan, as she encloses my breasts with warm, dry fingers, is stifled by our kissing. It's the most exciting sound. To hear my moans muffled in her mouth makes me feel high like little has before. She rolls my nipples between her fingers and tugs at them very gently. Before I can really delve into the thrills her caresses cause me, her hands have moved between my legs.

Her fingers act as if my panties aren't even there. She goes right for my most sensitive spot. I want to tell her that I need more stimulation, that I usually don't like my clit to be touched directly, but she's already flicking over it with her fingers.

There's something in my throat, a lump, a knot, fear, anticipation... I can't name it. A fluttering as if from tiny wings or words unspoken. It feels like the foreshadowing of something more, something big, something that will overwhelm me. With every smooth, slow touch, my ability to breathe lessens. There's a shallowness in my gasps that I can't control. It's as if my body refuses to take in the oxygen it needs, or as if it can't, but it doesn't matter. Between her apt fingers, I can feel my clit swollen and myself needy.

I yelp, and immediately, she moves slower. Much slower. Painfully slow. The beating of my heart is still increasing, and it pumps against my chest with such force that it scares me. I gulp for air and the knot in my throat bursts. I erupt, but instead of the scream I expected, my voice breaks into wobbly noises that sound like sobbing.

I thrash. I actually thrash around. I've never felt my body so aware, so alive to every nerve signaling through blinded senses. She doesn't stop her caress, and the throbbing blazes up again, carrying me to another dazzling high before I collapse into her arms.

My limbs, tired of fighting the water and heavy with satisfaction, cuddle against her. I'm hot, I'm burning. And I want to share that heat with her, I want to feel her naked in my arms. But even in my flaming state, I can feel the damp, chilly air creeping into her room and the draft breezing through the badly insulated balcony doors.

I press a kiss on her temple and take her hand. A shudder runs through my body as we leave the snug space of the couch, and we seek refuge underneath Felicity's blanket. It's as chilly and clammy as everything around us, and I only part from the sweater reluctantly. But then there's her naked body, her small breasts, and she feels so warm as she pulls me against her.

I straddle her and regard her body in the dim light. As I trail her neckline with my finger, I discover a dark little heart tattooed onto her left breast.

"Janis Joplin." She grins sheepishly. "She was my...my hero when I was in high school."

"And..."

"She had a tattoo like that."

There's so much I don't know about her.

I kiss the heart, and I kiss it again. I lay a little trail of kisses from the tattoo to her nipple, and I wrap my lips around it. I lick the salt off her skin. I press a kiss on her mouth, play with her tongue, and I know my fingers on her pussy catch her by surprise. I slide them between her folds and trace her flesh with my fingertips. She squirms underneath me, and there it is again, the thrilling sound of our moans, muffled by our lips.

The candle's flame flickers as I pull the cover over us, but it doesn't blow out. Darkness and the smell of Felicity's skin engulf me. I suck at her navel and my nipples graze her thighs. I want them in her mouth, I want to know how it feels like when she sucks at them and nibbles at them and licks and kisses them. But for now, there's her scent, and her wetness that I feel beneath my fingertips, and more than anything, I want to bury myself in it.

Much later, spooned by Felicity, I watch as the candle burns down. The smell of its smoke lingers in the air for a few moments. I hide a little grin in the pit of her arm as the thought crosses my mind that surely my mom hadn't had this situation in mind when she thought of me lighting it. Felicity stirs and rubs her nose against my neck, kissing my shoulder. She wraps her leg around mine and I can feel her pussy, warm and still wet, against me. My whole body is covered with a thin, invisible film, a sheen that is Felicity. I can taste its flavor on my lips. Felicity's kisses, her arousal, her touch, her tongue, her sweat, her scent.

I wriggle a bit deeper into her embrace, and I'm sure that we'll be a little awkward in the morning. That there will be a few giggles, especially on my part. Yet somehow I know that for the rest of our stay, I won't be making any more breakfasts for well-mannered guys, or getting jealous over doe-eyed girls stalking our kitchen.

HIGHER
LEARNING

Charlotte Dare

The week of midterms was an Indian summer scorcher. I sought refuge from the heat in the air-conditioned student center cafeteria, a dish of cold Sbarro spaghetti and meatballs for company. Sipping a Mountain Dew, I thought of how far I'd come since my first week on campus, shoulders stooped as I lugged an overstuffed book bag through the disinfected halls and lush grounds like a lost tourist in a foreign country.

Not only was I twice the age of the average student, I hadn't been in a classroom since most of them were in diapers. Quitting my full-time job to finish the BA I'd only got halfway through in a misspent young adulthood seemed like a good idea in theory since pushing claim denials at a health insurance company had lost its charm the week after I started eighteen years ago. But after the first desperate week of feeling overworked and over-whelmed, floating by the youthful masses as though I were a ghost, I had been ready to pack it in.

As I sat raking my fork through the pasty spaghetti,

congratulating myself on sticking it out this far, I noticed this cute kid hovering by the soft drink fountain. I'd look up, she'd look away and so on until the index cards I was memorizing for my chemistry midterm distracted me from our game. The next time I looked up, she was standing in front of me.

"Is anyone sitting here?" she asked.

I looked at the large table scattered with my books and note-book, lunch tray and dirty napkins, at the three empty chairs surrounding the table and then at her. "You mean besides me?"

Her wide smile revealed sparkling eyes obscured by the brim of her periwinkle university cap. "You mind if I sit? We're in the same chemistry class and I was wondering if you were having as much trouble memorizing this crap as I am."

I smiled back. "Look, just because I'm old doesn't mean I know everything. If you want to cheat off someone, I suggest you sit next to one of those science geeks that sit in the front of the lecture hall."

She won me with a childlike giggle. "You're not old," she said, sliding into the chair next to me. "And you're right—if I was looking to cheat, I would've picked one of the geeks."

"I'm old in comparison to everyone in class—that I know."

She scanned my face with scrutiny. "How old are you?"

"Thirty-nine," I said, sounding unnecessarily proud.

"That's not old. That's what we kids call a cougar." She winked and started nibbling on some granola from a Ziploc bag she pulled from the pocket of her pullover hoodie.

"Are you looking for a study buddy or are you hitting on me?"

She scratched under the brim of her cap and laughed, extending her hand. "I'm Jules, and I don't need help studying."

I clutched her warm hand. "I'm Corrine, and I'm not

interested in becoming the campus mascot, if you catch my drift. But thank you for the offer. It's the nicest one I've had all year."

She leaned forward and touched my forearm. "Seriously, I'm sorry about the cougar comment. That's not what this is about. I noticed you from the first day of class, and I just find you interesting."

"Well, thanks, Jules. It will be nice to have a friend around here."

Jules continued munching on her granola as I tried to resume studying. "You eat that stuff?" she asked after a long moment. She examined the plate of spaghetti like it was a science experiment.

"Certain sacrifices have to be made when you go back to college as an adult. Unfortunately for me, nutrition and taste are two of them."

She shook her head. "There's a great sushi hibachi downtown. Would you like to go there with me some time, like maybe this Saturday?"

"This Saturday?" I took off my reading glasses and addressed her earnestly. "How old are you, Jules?"

"Twenty-one. Why?"

"Why? You're twenty-one and beautiful and on a college campus full of other beautiful twenty-one-year-olds. You don't really want to have sushi with me."

"Uh, yeah, I do. That's kind of why I'm asking."

I thought about my ex, Maddy, and the look in her eyes when she denied she was leaving me for a twenty-eight-year-old Zumba instructor last year. I thought about the sense of rejection and the worthlessness that haunted me for months after she left. I thought about another weekend of either being a third wheel with my coupled friends or eating takeout alone in my apartment, and something other than common sense kicked in.

"Sure, Jules," I said with a sigh. "Let's go have sushi."

Her face beamed like the lights from the football field on game night, and I instantly considered rescinding my acceptance. But why not go? It was just dinner, and if I was going to be true to my resolution to be open to new experiences in my new life, I couldn't back down from this one.

She whipped out her iPhone. "Give me your cell. I'll call you and we can make the arrangements and such."

After I gave her my number, she bounced off through the cafeteria and smiled again at me just before she rounded the corner.

After our third Saturday trying out another sample of New Haven's multi-cultural fare, I realized that as much as I wanted to dismiss Jules as a "kid," I just couldn't. She was articulate, well-read and informed about nearly every current event I could throw at her. If I was going to find excuses for why I shouldn't be spending time with her, incompatibility certainly wasn't one of them.

"Why don't you park and come up for a while," she said, applying a fresh coat of peachy lip gloss. "You haven't even seen my dorm yet."

"Oh, that's okay. I wouldn't want to disturb your roommate."

"She's with her boyfriend every weekend. I always have the place to myself."

"Mmm, I don't know."

"Look, it's a decent little place. You'll like it." She paused for a moment and then looked at me with sweet, sad eyes. "Besides, it's not like you ever invite me to your place."

There it was, the conversation I had been hoping to avoid. We had been having a lovely time over the last three weeks getting to know each other—kissing only once the weekend before. But now came that inevitable, awkward nightcap moment, the consequence of which was that our relationship was going to change irrevocably. Honestly, I was enjoying spending time with her without any of that pressure.

"Okay, Jules, but I can't stay long."

"Suit yourself," she said and directed me toward the guest parking lot.

I glanced around her room at the tasteful Pier One Imports décor and wondered what I was doing there. Actually, I knew why I was there—Jules was irresistible, vibrant, sexy and apparently, attracted to me, if I was interpreting the footsies under the table at dinner correctly. But come on, Corinne, I thought, this can't possibly go anywhere. Wouldn't it end up being little more than a brief dalliance that would sap precious focus and energy I could be devoting to my studies?

Jules handed me a glass of chilled Riesling and before I could swallow the sip, her lips were on mine. All it took was a taste of those soft, luscious lips, like silky pillows, and I was done thinking and ready to respond to other instincts.

She led me toward the futon wedged between a desk and her roommate's bed, kissing me hard, biting my lips, tugging my bottom one with her teeth. I had forgotten what passion had felt like—or maybe I had never really known it, but what I was feeling with Jules was a complete awakening of every thought, emotion and nerve ending my body and spirit possessed.

I began caressing her sides, marveling at her firmness, the outline of her abdominal muscles as she moved. As badly as I wanted her, I sincerely hoped we would stop at kissing. What would she think of my body if she saw it or touched it? After Maddy left, I'd sort of let myself go and was only now on the way back to a comfortable weight. How could I, in good conscience, let this unsuspecting taut young woman know the real me?

She pulled me down on the futon and as we lay facing each other, smooching sensually, her hand crept up my shirt, over my sides and down my back.

"Let's keep it over the clothes, okay?" I said. "I'm sure I'm not what you're used to, and I wouldn't want you hit with any nasty surprises."

"What the hell are you talking about?"

I tried to sit up but she pulled me down on top of her.

"Corinne, you're amazing. Now will you please just kiss me?"

I wanted so badly to let go of my inhibitions—which by the way, I never knew I had until I'd started seeing this cougar-chasing co-ed.

She flicked open my bra with an expert snap of her fingers and grabbed hold of my breast, massaging my nipple with her thumb until her tongue took over. She sucked me until both nipples stood erect, wet and tingling, leaving her hand free to roam downward over my hip and across my stomach. She caressed me with her fingertips and then her nails and back to her fingertips, her hand dancing right above the waistband of my capri pants, her middle finger trying to ease its way inside. I was becoming so aroused sounds were escaping that I'd never heard myself make. Somehow she knew exactly how I wanted to be touched, all the while brushing her moist lips across mine.

She was tentative as her fingers slipped in through the side of my panties and gently rubbed and tickled my labia. She was making me so hot, I couldn't stand it anymore—I thought I'd come from the mere proximity of her hand.

"I want you, Corinne," she whispered in my ear. "Nobody's ever made me feel the way you do."

I kissed her harder, lost in the flattery, the passion, the throbbing in my pussy as her hand hovered near my clit.

She finally pulled my pants to my ankles and slid her fingers into my wetness. I whimpered as her middle finger glided over my clit for the first time and pleasure radiated through my entire body. I gently bit into her shoulder while she stroked me slowly and homed in on the exact spot, sending my pelvis into action, grinding into her hand as the pleasure grew nearly unbearable.

"How does that feel, baby?" she whispered in my ear, but I couldn't even speak.

With a climax I had only read about in erotica collections, she brought me to an orgasm that left me shuddering as I clung to her, nuzzling my face into her neck.

"Oh my god, Jules," I panted. "I can't believe how good that was."

"I'm so glad, Corinne," she whispered as she kissed my forehead.

In all the dozen years I'd been with Maddy and even in my prior relationships, I had never been made love to with such intensity and tenderness. I lay in her arms for I don't know how long afterward, waiting for her to make the subtle move indicating it was her turn, but she never did. She continued to hold me, kiss me and caress my forearms and hands like she was put on this earth to please me.

When I finally maneuvered her under me, she kissed me with such force I thought she might suck out my fillings. She smelled so fresh, like a summer picnic dessert, between the fruity hair product and coconut body lotion, and I couldn't wait any longer to taste her.

The thought of her roommate bebopping into the room and catching Jules in bed with a woman twice her age kept me awake the better part of the night. It was nearing some ungodly hour like five A.M. when I attempted to execute the escape plan I had hatched while lying entwined in a latticework of Jules's arms and legs.

My exit strategy was almost successful until I extracted the last toe from between her ankles. After all the writhing and shifting in that tiny bed, it was that one last stealth movement that betrayed me.

"Where are you going?" she asked, throaty with sleep.

Hmm, for which one would I opt: honesty or convenience?

"Uh, the bathroom." I was hopeless.

"It's two doors down. Hurry back, babe. I'm lonely without you."

I paused for a moment, my hand still on the knob. "Jules, I'm not going to the bathroom. I'm going home."

"What? Why?" She sat up and flipped on the lamp on her nightstand.

I exhaled deeply. "Look, I had a wonderful night with you, really, one I have to say I won't soon forget, but this just isn't going to work."

"How do you know?"

"Uh, well, forgive the condescension, but I have twenty years life experience on you. I've witnessed this type of impending doom with friends—I even went so far as to tell one she was a moron for not seeing what was so obvious to everyone else."

"I would think that someone with so much life experience would have learned not to generalize when it comes to matters of the heart." She tapped the spot on the bed I'd recently vacated.

I grinned at her. "You got me there. But you have to admit, this whole thing is pretty silly."

She sat up in bed and pulled the sheet up just above her

luscious handfuls of breasts. "What's silly? That we enjoy each other's conversation and had amazingly hot sex? Well, it was hot for me. Wasn't it hot for you?"

"Oh my god, Jules, it was incredible," I said as I wandered back to her bed. "And I do enjoy having dinner and talking with you. I just don't want any kind of emotional entanglements right now. I'm still trying to get my bearings on this new life I have without the added complication."

She contrived a massive frown and held out her hand to me. "I never wanted to be a complication in your life."

As I allowed her to pull me back into bed, I conjured the classic vision of being followed home by the wayward puppy dog. "What are you looking for, Jules?"

She wrapped her arms around me from behind and spooned me. "I wasn't looking for anything. In fact, if my plans come to pass, I'll be at the University of Maryland this time next year starting my MFA."

"Oh, then I guess I'm the silly one, forecasting this long, complicated love affair and you won't even be in Connecticut." I tightened up my fetal position.

"You're not silly," she said, hugging me closer to her. "I like the idea of having a love affair with you."

"I kinda like it, too," I conceded.

Once the kissing started, there was no time left to fall back to sleep. I was a little late and more than a bit drowsy for my eight A.M. Intro to Education lecture, but I didn't mind at all.

"One of these days we may actually get through this whole movie," I said, clicking off the DVD of *Love Affair* with Warren Beatty and Annette Bening.

"We almost made it," Jules said with a coy smile. "I'm afraid this time it was my fault. Sorry."

I crawled back under the covers as the rain poured down outside my apartment. "No need to apologize. I loved every minute of it."

"Are all thirty-nine-year-old women as passionate as you?"

"If they're all with girls as youthful and beautiful as you, I wouldn't hesitate to say yes." She flicked her tongue between my lips and smiled. "I can't believe you're leaving," I said. Sometimes I thought gazing into Jules's dreamy blues eyes afterward was my favorite part of making love.

"Maryland really isn't that far. We can do this, Cor. By the time you finish your BA and do your student teaching, I'll only have a couple of semesters left."

Caressing Jules's buttery-soft arms and thighs under the sheet as a summer breeze blew through my cracked window, I wanted so badly to say, "Yes, we can do it." It had been an amazing nine months—something so innocent and so unexpected, yet I knew my heart and my consciousness would never be the same. "That sounds nice, baby, but I think we should go ahead with my plan of going our separate ways and seeing how it goes."

"But I don't like that plan," she said. "I don't like thinking about my days and nights without you in them. Why can't we just stay together and see how it goes?"

"You have got to stop shooting down my iron-clad logic so effortlessly. You're starting to give me a complex."

She went quiet as she buried her face in my neck. I wrapped my arms around her and kissed the top of her head, thinking she was also savoring the ecstasy of lying in each other's arms— until I heard the sniffles. Oh, God, not the sniffles. Why did she always have to do that to me?

"What's the matter, baby?"

"I don't want to lose you."

"You won't lose me. We'll just have each other in a different way. We'll always be friends."

"I don't want you in a different way. I want you this way."

I wanted to squeeze the breath out of her. How did this happen? Why did it happen? The last thing I needed was to fall crazy in love with this beautiful person just beginning her life, and yet that was exactly what had happened. She filled me with an enthusiasm for life and love and a passion I hadn't known I was capable of feeling. And now our days together were slipping through our fingers like raindrops through the rhododendron blossoms outside my window.

"We'll be okay, Jules. It'll work out the way it's meant to," I told her, pressing her body close to mine.

"Promise me, Corinne."

"Promise," I whispered, but in my heart I knew the only promise I could make was that I'd always love her.

Suddenly, it was pouring inside as well.

Dropping her off at the train station that day in late August hit me harder than I'd expected, although Jules never knew it. She was so sensitive about leaving, especially in the days before her departure, that I really thought she was going to withdraw her enrollment and apply to our university's MFA program. But I discouraged it from the get-go. She had missed her family back in Maryland for the last four years, and I told her she would regret not following through with her original plans.

"You're sure you won't forget me?" she asked before getting out of my car.

"Baby, I couldn't forget you if I wanted to." I caressed her cheek, soft and still tanned from our last beach trip to Hammonasset State Park. "And believe me, I don't want to."

"And you're going to text me, right?"

"Of course I will."

"And I'm coming up next month the weekend of the twentieth, right?"

"You better," I said with a quiet smile. "I'll be waiting."

She exhaled deeply and clutched my hand in hers. "I'm afraid you're going to fall in love with someone your own age."

"I'm afraid you will, too." At that point I had to glance out my side window. "But that's okay if you do. I'll understand."

"I won't understand if you do." She threw her arm around my neck and kissed my cheek down to the bone. "Yes, I will."

We said our *I love yous*, about a dozen altogether, and kissed until our lips were dry. She moved slowly down the sidewalk toward the train station, lazily swinging her two duffel bags at her sides. My stomach tightened as she approached the entrance, and I hoped she wouldn't look back.

KAT'S HOUSE

Mia Savage

My shift ended at eleven. It had been a good night; no one went to jail and I was still alive. I changed into street clothes, grabbed my jacket and helmet and headed for my Harley.

"Want to grab a bite, Lynn?" Michelle yelled from the elevator.

"Got to go. Kate's cooking tonight."

I drove home trying to figure out what Kate had planned. Our first anniversary had been a very nice, romantic dinner. We made love until sunrise. *I could do that again for number two.*

Apparently, my girlfriend had other plans. Taped to my front door was a large white printed card, guaranteeing something was going to be different about *this* anniversary. It was some sort of menu, complete with a fancy logo. *The Kat House.*

I stared at the words.

Appetizer
Entrée
Dessert

Each had a list of shocking options.

How could she know? *What* did she know? There was only one way to find out.

I opened the door and entered another world, a world I had only dreamed about. Everything in our living room was different—walls draped with black velvet fabric, furniture layered with satin and fur throws, pillows everywhere. Soft sultry jazz music and candlelight completed the mood.

Kate stood in the living room doorway. She looked completely different from the woman I had kissed good-bye this morning before leaving for work. Tonight, she wore a black tuxedo jacket with long tails and satin lapels. It opened in the front to a V closing just under her belly button...*ring?* The small gold hoop was new too.

I flicked it with a fingertip. "Very sexy."

"Welcome to *The Kat House,* I'm Kat," she said, her voice low and sultry.

Leading me to the large leather chair we cuddled in to watch television, she said, "Please, have a seat. May I remove your boots?"

"Yes." My heart was pounding. I had gone from mild worry to feverish lust in mere seconds.

I sat back as she knelt and placed the sole of my boot against her thigh. Unzipping it, she never took her beautiful, mischievous eyes off mine. She slid first one boot off, then the other. I still couldn't believe this was happening.

Kate handed me the same cup of coffee she gave me every night when my shift ended, but tonight she did it in sheer black stockings and mile-high heels. She grinned a naughty grin.

"Enjoy your coffee. I'll be right back." She turned gracefully and walked away, the split in the tails of her jacket exposing her beautiful ass.

I sat back, feeling like this was a dream I was in no hurry to awaken from. I couldn't wait to see what she had planned next. The menu had only hinted at the possibilities; I was eager to see how far she would really take this.

This was the same woman I knew intimately, and yet she was acting like a stranger. We'd met when I pulled her over for a broken taillight and ended up offering to fix it for her. She tartly informed me as she accepted the warning citation, in her two-hundred-dollar tailored suit, that she was perfectly capable of fixing the bulb herself. It was love at first fight. I apologized, asked her to have dinner with me and the rest is history.

Before I could wrap my head around it all, she reappeared carrying a silver tray. She sat on the ottoman in front of me, the tray on her lap. Her erect nipples poked at the fabric covering them. I wanted to touch her, to take control as I had longed to do for so long, but I wanted to draw it out. To be sure.

"Would you like a snack?" She waved her hand over an assortment of fruits, cheeses and crackers, beautifully displayed.

I reached for a chocolate-covered strawberry.

"Please, allow me to serve you." She held the succulent-looking berry up to my lips. As the silky chocolate and luscious fruit slid over my tongue, I imagined it was her.

She kissed my lips clean when I was finished, then sat back again, an expectant look on her face. "Are you ready for your appetizer?"

"Ready? I've never been so ready for anything."

"I apologize for making you wait."

"It's okay," I started to say, before thinking better of it. This was my chance to change things with us forever. She was giving me the long-awaited green light.

Lap Dance... A tantalizing treat sure to arouse the senses.

"I'll have the lap dance."

With a nod, she lifted the stereo remote and changed the music, turning up the volume until it pulsed. Standing in the spread of my thighs, she swayed her hips to the seductive rhythm.

Her slow, deliberate motions hypnotized me. I loved this new bad-girl attitude.

She pushed her hips forward, moving closer to me as I fought my insatiable urge to touch her when she dropped her jacket to the floor. She cupped her breasts, taunting me.

My pussy throbbed and my jeans pressed my pubic bone, adding fuel to the already raging fire building between my legs, making me squirm. I couldn't take it anymore.

"Come here." I reached for her, using her hips to pull her down to grind my moist denim into her saturated silk. I grasped her breasts in my hands and kissed her perfumed neck.

She pushed her pussy against mine while she rode my large silver belt buckle.

"Not so fast," I said, catching her wrists behind her and pulling her back.

"Finish my dance," I demanded, feeling both a bit strange and empowered. I ached to do to her what I had only read about. I wanted to possess her. Take her. Push her.

The whole thing scared me a little, really. I wasn't a mean person. Why had she brought out urges in me that no one had before? Now was not the time to worry about it, I decided. It was finally happening, and I was going to make the most of it.

Lifting herself from my lap, she continued her seduction of my mind and body. My lust was now almost painful. I tugged down on the legs of my jeans to alleviate the pressure against my throbbing clit.

When the music faded, she picked up her jacket. "Are you ready for your entrée?"

Was she rushing because she was nervous, or was she mad I hadn't let her come?

"Well?" she said, her usual impatience finally getting the better of her.

"I'll let you know when I'm ready." My tone was firm, but inside I grinned, eager to see how she'd handle that.

Her eyes flashed, but taking a deep breath, she nodded.

I sat back, enjoying the moment. Taunting her was pleasurable, but imagining how beautiful she was going to be bound and helpless, I wanted her so badly I wasn't sure I would be able to hold out for my own fantasy.

I reached for her. She took a step back, just beyond my reach.

I stood, lightning fast after years of police training, grabbed her wrist and pulled her against me. "Don't ever pull away from me. If you don't want to do this, say so now."

I could see the play of emotions on her face as the weight of what she was offering sank in. Was she truly ready to take our commitment to another level?

"Time-out, Kate."

"What? Don't stop. I want this. Please."

"No stopping, unless you say so. Say *time-out* and I swear I will stop."

She grinned. *Time-out* was what she always said if I was ranting about work. "Perfect."

"Good, now that we've settled that, just stand there and be still," I hissed in her ear before releasing her as abruptly as I had grabbed her.

She shivered, and though she remained silent, her expressive eyes spoke volumes. They told me the story of her lust, fear and anticipation.

"Tonight, we'll test your will and my control." I felt a surge of power run through me.

I placed both of her hands in the small of her back, pulling her to me in one motion. She stiffened, leaning against me. Her breath was hot on my skin.

She whispered, "Kiss me." Her moist lips begged, but her eyes challenged.

"I'll kiss you when I'm ready."

She smiled. "I think you're ready now." She freed her hands and slid her fingers over my damp crotch.

"I. Said. Not. Now." I turned her around with a tug on her wrists.

She stumbled for balance. I steadied her back against my chest. Pulling her arms behind her, I gripped them both in my left hand, then pushed her forward to admire her rear view.

She always wore sexy lingerie, but nothing quite this naughty before. The black lace garter belt clung to her curvy hips, displaying her round bottom exposed by a barely-there thong.

"Stay here. Do not move and do not turn around." I smacked her ass to accentuate my instructions, bending her arms so her entangled fingers rested again on the small of her back.

Met with hesitation, I squeezed her delicate wrists tighter. "Do you understand?"

I knew this would be hard for her, my proud, in charge Kate.

"Yes." The word seemed to catch in her throat as she coughed.

"What was that?"

"Yes!"

"Good. That was the last time I ask you twice. Are we clear?"

"Yes."

I released her hands, pleased to see they remained where I had placed them as I walked to the table by the front door. I rummaged in my saddlebag, quickly finding the items I needed.

She jerked when I clamped the hard steel handcuff around her right wrist but did not protest when I secured the left.

I turned her to face me and kicked the inside of her feet with mine to spread them, my eager fingers cupping the saturated silk patch between her legs.

She took in a shattered breath as I ran a moist trail up to her navel. I teased the small gold loop that had replaced her usual diamond stud, pulling and releasing it just beyond comfort. Her body tightened against the pain, then pressed forward as if anticipating the next tug.

Every reaction taught me something new.

I tweaked her nipples and used them to pull her to me. She arched her back, and her head fell backward. I squeezed and twisted her nipples, softly at first, then increased the pressure until she moaned. I pulled one breast upward and leaned down slightly to meet it with my mouth.

She pressed closer and I moved to her other breast. I took all I wanted, then moved back to the first before blowing a cool breath over her ripe flesh.

I leaned in close to her ear again. "Is this what you wanted?" My breath tousled a small strand of hair escaping its own bondage near her earlobe.

She just looked at me, refusing to answer yet again.

I abruptly turned her to face the chair, then pushed her forward over the high, plush arm. Her ass was prominently displayed.

Her face was buried in the thick cushion. I caressed her tender skin until her tight muscles relaxed and her breathing returned to normal.

When I landed my first firm smack across her unsuspecting asscheek, she rose up only to be forced back down by my hand between her shoulder blades. "Is there a problem, Princess?" She hated the nickname.

"No." Her voice was muffled but her response quick.

Her hands lay in the small of her back, fists clenched. I ran my fingernails across the slight red spot my smacks had left behind. She wiggled her hips, whether asking for more or trying to get away, I did not know.

I drew back and landed another loud swat in the same location, then another, increasing my firing rate.

Her motion increased with each landing. Her skin grew redder. My hand got hotter with each contact. Her moans grew louder and seemed to come from somewhere deep within her.

I scraped her discolored flesh with the tips of my fingers, then reached into my front pocket and drew out a blade.

She stiffened at the sound of the knife clicking open. "Don't move," I said.

One quick slice and the strings of her thong were severed, exposing her flushed, damp skin and the valley between her spread thighs. I placed my fingers at the edge of her pulsing desire.

She pushed her pussy to me, as if begging for my fingers' penetration. I pushed two fingers deep inside her, then pulled out quickly. She groaned, wiggling in frustration.

"Beautiful," I said, wrapping my fingers around the bun on the back of her head, using it to urge her back to her feet.

I pulled her firmly against me, her hands trapped helplessly between us; her neck stretched back, head held to my shoulder. My large hand wrapped around her throat. Her rapid pulse under my fingertips combined with her utter surrender to me made me feel truly in control of her.

She pushed her ass back against me. "Please. Please."

"Please what, Princess?" I loosened my grip on her throat.

"Please, touch me."

"I am touching you. Feel me now?" I squeezed a bit harder on the pulsing arteries of her neck, my emergency assistance training telling me exactly how much pressure was enough to torment her without actually putting her in any danger. As she lost her will to struggle, I overflowed with love for this newly born, helpless creature. I loosened my grip, and she remained still and quiet against me.

"Did I say you could relax?"

"No," she answered, quicker this time.

I pushed her forward and smacked her ass a couple more times. She stood awaiting my next action, as submissive as could be. I was amazed by her natural ability at something I thought she had known nothing about.

"Lean over the chair," I said.

This time, there was no hesitation. I kicked her feet as far apart as I could get them, leaning in and plunging two fingers into her hot pussy.

Her strong muscles pulled me in and squeezed me back out, tighter and stronger with each thrust into her. I penetrated her deeper than I could ever remember. Her walls tightened around me, and I thrust my hips toward her, forcing more of my hand into her willing cunt.

She pushed back against me, her body begging me to give her more. I pulled my dripping fingers out. My burning desire to clutch the tender meat of her ass overwhelmed me, and I squeezed hard, which made her twist away again. Her rebellion inflamed my desire to punish her, and to control her. I grabbed the silky hair between her legs and pulled her upward for better access.

"Are you sure this is what you want, Princess? I could stop. Right now."

"Yes, please. I mean no! Please, don't stop."

I replied by shoving as much of my hand as I could into her tight pussy. Her body convulsed and she pleaded for more, coming and coming, giving and taking more than I had ever thought possible.

"There's no escape this time. No stopping just this side of the line."

She writhed as I kept up the barrage of swipes to her clit, then back into her now soaked and throbbing cunt. Grinding my pussy into her lush ass drove my fingers deeper into her. I came. My release flashed through me like an electrical storm on a hot summer afternoon, soaking my jeans through from inside and out. I squeezed her tenderized ass as I rode it out.

"Please," she pleaded again, "please stop."

I continued my assault until she went limp and my own senses returned. I took the handcuff key from my pocket and released only one of the bracelets, scooping her up in my arms and holding her while the aftershocks rippled through her.

I carried her to our bed and cuffed her to the headboard, crawling in beside her. As long as I kept her captive, this dream would not have to end.

"Happy anniversary," she whispered.

"You still owe me dessert," I said, chuckling.

She laughed, snuggling up closer as I wrapped my arms around her. "Just wait until you see the breakfast menu."

GUISE
AND DOLLS

Allison Wonderland

I'm not a big fan of coffee, but I could really go for a cup of Jo.

Just look at her. She's... Oh, you can't. Well, that's okay. I'll look and you look forward to my risqué yet respectful descriptions.

If she were a dyke, Jo would be the ultimate lipstick lesbian. She certainly has the face for it: pretty and painted and perfect. And she definitely has the figure for it: Jo's got more curves than a crazy straw. She even wriggles when she walks, except she doesn't walk—she struts, hips swiveling like a hula dancer, legs flexing like a ballet dancer. When she struts across campus, the guys say, "Looking good today, Joelle," as if she didn't look good yesterday and might not look good tomorrow. Everywhere she goes, she is besieged by winks and whistles and overtures of fornication.

That's because everywhere she goes, everyone thinks she's straight. And she is. Just look at her. I know—you can't. You'll have to trust me on this one. Everything about her is straight: her teeth, her posture, her hair, her orientation.

Speaking of orientation, that's when I first laid thighs on her. We're both... What? I said eyes. All right, I meant to say eyes. Anyway, we're both students in the Conservatory of Theatre Arts. I thrive on dyke drama, which is why I'm in the Dramatic Writing program. Joelle is a drama queen of a different sort— she's majoring in Performance. During freshman orientation last semester, the Wellness Center put on a bunch of hokey health skits about stress and sex and other collegiate concerns. Joelle was one of the actors in a play called, "You Booze, You Lose... Your Virginity." She turned in a pretty good performance. Not exactly a tour de force, but even I got a little misty.

"For crying out loud, this is so ridiculous," Joelle remarks as we make our way toward the dorms. She's not strutting now; she's stomping—stomping across the brick tiles that pave the campus. This place is such an eyesore. All the buildings are brown, like an old-timey radio. It seems like the only campus beautification project the school has undertaken is admitting Joelle. She could beautify... Sorry, I didn't mean to interrupt.

"I'm supposed to tear up at the end of 'Adelaide's Lament,'" Joelle laments. "Adelaide's all groom and doom because the guy she's in love with doesn't want to take the plunge, so she develops this miserable cold, yada yada. I have to go from sick sniffles to sob sniffles. The problem is I can't fake it; I have to feel it. Well, I would if I could but I can't, so... I can't. It's such a far cry from what I—" Loose tiles rattle like dishes and I snatch Jo's arm when she wobbles. "If my acting career fails, the only thing I have to fall back on is my ass."

I study the snug hug of Jo's shorts—a little too longingly, because I'm starting to feel that customary quiver. I push my spiral notebook up against my chest so that if my body decides to broadcast my craving for Jo to the entire student body, it won't look like I'm smuggling gumdrops under my shirt.

"Sure, I've gotten worked up over somebody before," Joelle is saying, "but it's different with...you know."

"With Brent?" I venture, following Joelle into the residence hall.

"Uh, no. Brent is bent."

"Why? Because he's in the thee-ay-ter?"

"No, because he's gay. You think every guy is after me. I'm—" Joelle unlocks the door to her suite and waves me ahead. "After you. I'm not the Big Woman on Campus, or whatever the female equivalent would be. Is there one?"

"Beats me." I stretch out on Jo's bed, the closest I'll ever come to sleeping with her. Her sheets smell like a gingerbread house. I rub my bare legs against the cotton. "And FYI, Joelle, every guy is after you."

"Oh, yeah?" Jo sets her script onto the desk beside the intro to anthro textbook. "Name one."

"Darrin."

"Darrin?"

"That guy who was in the elevator with us at the Student Center yesterday. Darrin took one look at you and was instantly bewitched."

Jo's eyebrows curve like rainbows. "Like you?"

I shift on the bed, my elbows thrusting against the mattress, which is ludicrously long and makes me feel puny and pitiful. I'm blushing, too, I can tell—the closet is across from the bed and the door is one big mirror. "Like anyone."

Jo slides the closet door open and for one merciful moment the mirror disappears. "Don't undress me with your lies," she says, selecting a pair of jeans on a silly satin hanger. "You're more transparent than a pair of pantyhose." She slides the door closed, forcing me to come face-to-face with the numskull in its reflection. "You're also weirdly interested in men," Joelle adds. She takes the jeans off the hanger. "What were you like B.C.?"

"B.C.?"

"Before cunt. Or did you always prefer pu...dding?"

"You can say *cunt* but not *pussy*?" I tease, only mildly mortified now.

Joelle kneels down, ducking her head so that her hair hides her ketchup-colored complexion. "*Cunt* is more distinguished," she mumbles, fussing with one of the many straps that trap her feet inside her shoes. The V-neck of her shirt dips into a U.

"I'll do it." I practically throw myself at her feet.

Joelle stands. "It's nice to have friends in low places."

Friends. Why did I pursue a friendship with Jo when I can't pursue a romance with her? I mean, what is it about unrequited love that makes it so appalling and appealing at the same time? I hope the professor covers this topic in my Psychology of Women course. Otherwise, I may have to withdraw. "Um, B.C. To answer your question, I dated guys during that epoch, but I always knew I liked the birds better than the bees, so... Hmm. I think only half that euphemism is effective, but you get the gist."

Jo steps out of her shoes. "So did you ever let a bee sting you?"

"Nope." I flop back onto the bed, the pleats in my skirt spreading out like a paper fan.

"I think I'm allergic to bees," Jo says, unbuttoning her shorts. She grins at me. Looking away is not an option. "You've seen London. You've seen France. Now you get to see my—"

"Camouflage underpants? Who do you think you are—G.I. Jo?" I'm surprised they're so simple, but they're sexier that way: no frills, just thrills.

Joelle trades in her shorts for the pair of pants she got from her closet. She leads them up her legs, slowly concealing their svelte shape with the dark denim.

"Do these jeans make my ego look fat?" Joelle inquires, posing like a paparazzi princess in front of the mirror.

"Colossal." I pat her posterior. "Just like your caboose."

Joelle shakes her ass in my face. "You can borrow them sometime."

"Oh, so you're going to let me get in your pants?"

"Absolutely."

My smile squirms. "Stop leading me on," I mutter, half-hoping she'll hear me and half-hoping she won't. It's my fault—I shouldn't be flirting with Jo, not when she knows I have feelings for her. And she knows. There's no way she can't know. It's plain as gay. Day. Whatever.

"I'm not leading you on," Jo insists, but her tone is too chirpy, like she doesn't take me seriously.

"You're a leading lady. It's what you do."

"I'm not always a leading lady. Freshman year I auditioned for Peggy Sawyer in *42nd Street*, but they cast me as Dorothy Brock. It all worked out for the best, though, since Dorothy has this fabulous song about wanting someone to be gay with, to play with. Not exactly your garden variety coming-out story, is it?"

Jo wants someone to be gay with? Great. Jo wants to play with someone? "Great, I'm in love with a playgirl."

"Luck, be a lady. You're in love with me?"

"Like you didn't know." Atta girl—make her look stupid.

"I knew you were attracted to me, but I didn't know your heart was involved, too."

She's next to me on the bed, smiling with her straight teeth and sitting with her straight spine and...and... "Not exactly your garden variety coming-out story?"

"Hey, just because my posture is straight doesn't mean that I am."

"But you look so—"

"Ladylike?"

"Yeah." Stupid Sapphic stereotypes.

"You look ladylike, too, except when you sit like that." She studies my signature sprawl. "Look at you. Legs spread. Wide open. Gaping. Legs. Wide open."

"Hey, just because I'm not sitting pretty doesn't mean that I'm—"

"A lesbian?"

"Yeah. Wait, what?"

"Sometimes you're more bewildered than bewitched." Jo jabs my side like she's trying to stick a straw into a juice box. It tickles then tingles. "I hate that about you."

"Is there anything that you love about me?"

She shrugs her shoulders. "Nothing."

"What else?"

She hugs my shoulders. "Everything."

I stare at Jo. Unblinking, unthinking.

"Oh, come on," she says, "you think I've been flirting with you all this time for tits and giggles?"

"I don't know. I guess. Sort of. Maybe?"

"Okay, clearly you didn't like that question, so maybe you'll like this one: What does a person have to do to get some lip service around here?"

Nothing, apparently—before I can do or say anything, Joelle is shoving her fingers into my hair, letting them tangle in the loopy blond locks. I guess gentlemen aren't the only ones who prefer blondes.

I delight in the sensations. The kiss is long and long overdue.

It is liberal and liberating, decadent yet decorous. Jo's lips taste like tropical punch and her mouth tastes like blueberry yogurt. She's a remarkable kisser, and I'm not just saying that because I'm in love with her. She kisses with precision, perfection, panache.

But then, I figured she would.

She's not your average Jo.

Joelle slams the door of my room. The bulletin board above my desk shudders. The framed poster beside my bed—Marilyn Monroe lifting weights in blue jeans and the top half of a bikini—jiggles.

"Most people go out with a bang," I remark, retrieving a fallen flyer for Jo's show. "Not you. You come in with one."

"Your roommate isn't here, is she?"

I scan the room: bunk bed, books, basket full of garments that just got back from a trip to the laundry room. But no room- mate. "She's in class. Well, she could be in the closet, but let's not go there." Jo rolls her eyes. I close my laptop. "What's up?"

"The curtain," she says, dropping into a blue plastic chair that feels more comfortable than it looks.

"You've got four hours till show time."

"I'm not going on."

"Yes, you are."

"Not in my condition." She sniffles. "I think I'm coming down with something."

"You're too hot to catch cold." Jo is the first to growl at me. Her stomach goes next. "You hungry?"

"I'm too nervous to eat."

I slide my desk chair back and make the brief migration to the other side of the room. I kneel in front of Jo, folding my arms over her thighs. "We'll get your favorite: spaghetti SOS."

"That's not a bad idea, actually. I could use all the help I can get."

"Not help, silly. SOS. Sauce on the side."

Jo starts to smile, then stops. "Don't be endearing. I can't handle it right now."

"How come you're so nervous?"

"My mind is a tabula rasa. I can't remember diddly." She taps her foot, starts singing the bushel and a peck song, groping for the words.

"Isn't there something about hugging and necking?" I query, and get a weary look in response. Maybe I should show, not tell. I lift myself onto Jo's lap and wrap my arms around her neck, nuzzling her manicured mane, dark and shiny like black coffee. "I know what you need." Reluctantly, I climb off Jo's thighs and move to stand behind her. "You need a massage," I offer, rubbing her shoulders.

Joelle shrugs against my hands. "I don't think that will be sufficient," she says. "I do, however, think that I'm going to faint."

I frown down at her. "Put your head between your legs."

Jo frowns up at me. "So when I pass out I can hit my head on the floor? Do I look like a numskull to you?" She slants her head to one side, her eyes narrowing into buttonholes. "Can't you put your head between my legs?"

A fuzzy feeling flutters inside my panties. "You want me to give you a peck on your bushel?" My heart socks my rib cage and my knees knock together like a plastic clacker. But I'm not too nervous to eat.

I come around the front of the chair and kneel at Jo's feet again. I curl her skirt up across her thighs. No camouflage panties today. No panties period.

It takes a moment for my eyes to adjust, as if someone's just switched on a light in a dark room. I peruse her pussy, all lush lips and liquid lust. Her curls are pitch-black, like the flats and sharps of a piano, and curve like the binding of a spiral notebook.

My tongue traces every crest and crinkle of her pussy, follows every flavorful fold of her cunt. She tastes like Bartlett pears and conversation hearts—succulent and sugary.

"You're getting wet," Jo remarks.

My head pops up like a periscope from between her thighs. "How do you know?"

"Your hair's in the dip."

I glide my hand through my tresses. Smeared strands stick to my fingers. I grip the tips, massage the gel into the blond loops.

Joelle's lips skew into a half smile, as if she's too worn out to lift up the other side of her mouth. "That's one way to treat split ends," she mumbles.

I duck back down. Whispered whimpers glide past Jo's lips and she grinds her groin against my mouth.

"I'll know when my love comes a—" I murmur into her sex.

"Adelaide doesn't sing that number," Jo grouses, her voice deep and drowsy.

"I'll know when my love comes."

"Now you've got my number." Joelle kicks like a chorus girl. I hold her thighs tighter, my nails scraping her skin like a pencil scratching across paper. I look up. Joelle's eyes are half-lidded and she's making this hum-cum-moan sound.

"That was nicely-nicely done," she says, looking satisfied.

Perhaps a little too satisfied.

"You weren't nervous at all, were you?" I query. "You conned me into cunnilingus." Jo giggles. "You stooped pretty low, you know that?"

"I know. But, hey, at least I didn't stoop as low as you did." She grins at me, her mermaid-green eyes sparkling. I gaze into them, watching as they begin changing color like autumn leaves—except instead of getting lighter, they're getting darker.

Jo sweeps me off my feet, dragging me to the bottom bunk, which, fortunately, is mine and not my roommate's.

She sprawls on top of me, assuming a most unladylike position. She kisses me—intimate but insistent. Her hand moves over my hip, onto my thigh, under my skirt, inside my panties.

She dips her fingers into the steam bath and gasps. "It's like a sauna in there," she murmurs.

Jo lets her fingers soak for a while. I squeeze her breasts, the cups plump and cushy against my palms.

Things start to heat up. Jo strokes and pokes and stokes until the steam hisses and blasts.

"It's too bad you didn't audition for the show," she remarks, almost as breathless as I am.

She offers her fingers.

Her skin is sticky and slippery and sweltering.

I can take the heat.

"You would have made the perfect Hot Box Girl."

TAMAGO

Anna Watson

"I love butch women because it was butch sexual response that gave me my body."

—Carol Queen

"When I found butch/femme it was like rediscovering my heart through my cunt."

—Amber L. Hollibaugh

"I want to bring out the girl in you. I want to be your butch. I've got your number, doll."

—A cowboy

Beautiful

It's morning in Sheffield, Iowa, sometime in the early sixties. I'm probably about eight, visiting for the summer. My grandmother is getting dressed in front of the big mirror in the bathroom. I'm sitting on the closed toilet, watching, because at my house, with my no-nonsense mom, nothing this exciting ever happens. Grandmimi pulls on pantyhose, a slip. Her skirt, the matching blouse. A pin, bracelet, her rings. She steps into her high, high heels. Fluffs up her hair, nails it with hair spray. Spritzes perfume. She uses an eyelash curler, mascara, powder, rouge. And finally, she untubes her red lipstick and deftly colors her lips. Now I'm standing next to her. She knows I'm down here, by her hip. She tears herself away from her fabulous reflection to swoop down in a cloud of perfume and hair spray for my morning kiss, full on the lips. Now I'm beautiful, too.

TURNED ON
We're all at the counter of a local health food place, having a smoothie after class. I'm in graduate school with more lesbians than I've known my whole life. The class is even taught by a lesbian! Naomi is on one side of me, Beth on the other, and we're supposed to be discussing a group project. I've only been out a little while and am living with a girl I met in a support group for bisexual women, but she's nothing like these two. Naomi is a redhead, freckled, athletic, pushy, flirty. Beth is blond, smaller, more intellectual, shy. Butch. They're both so butch. All of a sudden, a flush rises up my body, and I'm blushing, apropos of nothing we're talking about. I laugh and hold my cheeks and say, "Gosh, I don't know why talking about this project is making me blush like this!" They look at me, grinning.

EGG
In Japan, if you're a neophyte at something, you're called an egg. When you first enter a company, for example, before you learn all the ropes, you're an egg. *Tamago.* New, smooth, waiting to hatch. I'm an egg at being femme. Dani says I'm doing things

right, that the femme/butch vibe is there, but I sure don't have a
lot of experience. I say, "Don't be mad if I do the wrong thing.
I'm just an egg." She says, "I like your eggness." I know being
femme is what makes the breath blow out of me when she calls
and says, "Babe, I just wanted you to know that I was driving
along here, thinking about your breasts." Being femme is my
hand on her bicep. Undoing her tie when we're making out in
her truck. Hiking up my skirt and lowering myself onto her dick
as she lies on the bed, that look on her face.

TRUCK

We met online and even after weeks of emails and phone calls,
I was nervous about telling her my address, so on our first date,
Dani picks me up on Mass Ave., in front of the barbeque place.
Her old Ford truck idles at the curb. She says she watched me in
the rearview mirror as I walked up. Says she could tell I was all
femme when I rounded the corner. I have never dated a butch
before and am just coming out of a lesbian relationship, just
coming into my femme self. Her words feed me. We've been
driving maybe ten minutes when I ask if there's a seat belt in the
middle. There is, and I move over next to her, just like boys and
girls drive the backroads all over the Midwest, close together.
After that, I always ride in the middle. I love how she holds the
buckle up for me, already to my width. These little things, these
things men used to do for women and women rebelled against
and now I want so deeply from her. To feel cherished by her. To
feel myself in her hands.

DATE

"This is your date," she tells me when we're driving one night.
"We can find a restaurant and have supper, or I can pull over and
fuck you silly." Guess which one I pick? After I start breathing

again, that is. We end up in the parking lot of an urban beach, a place where gay guys are cruising each other. I'm nervous; I've never had sex outside of a house before. What if a cop car comes up? What if a carload of bashers drives in? I can tell Dani is on alert the whole time she's doing me, the whole time her skilled fingers are dicking in and out of me and sweet, dirty words are tumbling from her lips. "There's a guy cruising me," she whispers. "He would be so surprised if he came over and saw who I've got in here, flat on her back." And then she says, in the same quiet tone, "Come now."

MY FIRST DICK

"This is my harness," she says. She's very matter-of-fact about this, but I'm so wound tight I can hardly sit still. She undoes one side, picks up the dildo. "And this is the dick I've chosen for you." It's obsidian black, circumcised, fatter at the base.

"It's big!" I choke out.

"Too big, baby?" She's looks concerned.

"I don't know. We'll have to see."

She nods. She's so serious. "I chose this one for you," she says, notching it into the ring, "because, after having had my fingers inside you, he's the one I think will fit you best."

He? Is that how butches talk about their dicks? I can feel it in my stomach when she talks about having her fingers inside me. How will it feel to have her dick there? And how bizarre that someone can choose a dick for you! The guys I've fucked over the years certainly never had that option; crooked, small, thick or slim, they were stuck with theirs for life. Dani currently has about seven of them, she says, all colors, but this is the only one I've seen, the one she chose for me. Once when we were talking on the phone, she told me she was boiling all her dicks on the stovetop to clean them, a multicolored stew, devoted to fucking.

WILLING

She answers my ad, which is titled "Willing." We've fucked three times, only once with the dildo. Her dick has had a profound effect on me. More than getting off. It's gotten inside my head. She emails, in her courtly way, "A willing Femme is a wonderful lay. I'm looking forward to having you in my arms again."

EGG AND STONE

We're in Dani's bedroom, standing in front of the mirror. Dani holds me from behind. She wants me to touch her but she's hesitant. She hasn't been naked with me before. The first time she fucked me with her dick, she was wearing all her clothes, including her boots. She lifts my shirt over my head and runs one finger up and down my breast, that secret, sexy smile on her face.

"What allows you to let me touch your body like this?" she asks, brushing my nipple. The light is bright in her room. My breasts are large, drooping, striated with stretch marks. They make me want to close my eyes, but the sight of Dani's hands stroking them doesn't allow it. I say, "Leap of faith."

"Yes," she says, and tells me what a precious gift it is for her to be able to touch a woman's body, how she comes to it in a sacred way, hoping the woman will know how trustworthy she is, how grateful.

"Hypocrite," I say softly, thinking how she hasn't trusted me to give to her in this way yet. After a long time she nods.

"You're right."

But she wants it. Bad. I don't mean she wants to be fucked, but she wants my hands on her body. She wants to be ministered to, as much as any do-me princess. I turn off the light and she shucks her boxers, practically running to the bed. She gets on her belly. She is so beautiful. I take out my tools but start with my fingers. Sometimes lovers get bored with this, she told me, when she was explaining to me about her desire. Yeah, yeah, you like your back and arms stroked, ho hum. I'm not bored. It's still sex. As I stroke Dani's back with my fingertips and watch her skin shudder, watch goose bumps rise on her arms, I remember how, when I was little, my girlfriends and I used to tickle each other's feet, stretched out on my bed, limp with sweetness. We scratched each other's backs, too. Long moments spent tickling, scratching, petting. Sometimes we would trace the alphabet with our fingers. "What letter is this?" It was never as easy to guess as you thought it was going to be.

Dani moves and moans under my hands. Sometimes she kicks her foot on the bed and I am startled, but she says it's a good kick. I take my first tool, a soft-haired paintbrush. "What is that?" she asks. "It feels so good!" I paint sensation up and down, side to side. She has told me how enjoyable the anticipation from one spot to the next is. I try to keep her guessing. Beside me on the bed are: a cotton ball, a powder puff, a feather, more paintbrushes of different widths and softness, rhododendron leaves, a daisy, a pinecone, a pine branch. As I try each one, relishing the different sounds they elicit, I flash on Dani as a sensuous, texture-hungry forest creature, half-buried in loam and moss and fallen leaves. I want to peel the wet leaves off her body one by one, discover with tongue and fingers the revealed flesh.

"What?" she asks. I've stopped, my hands resting lightly on her ravenous skin.

"Nothing," I say, moving again. "I was just thinking about leaves."

MARRIED
Tex and I started dating around the time Dani was shutting down on me, when things started to get just that smidge too

intimate for her. From pure fucking we'd gone to long, drawn-out conversations so convoluted I barely remember them later, save for the sad confused feeling they leave me with. Clearly our salad days were over. Back on butch-femme.com, I find Tex. The first time we talk on the phone, I think, *This butch is the marrying kind*, and seven years later we're walking down the aisle.

Tex isn't jealous of Dani. "I'm grateful to that guy," she says when we talk about it. "She took the edge off for me. You might have been too much for me to handle when you first got your femme going."

On our honeymoon night at the Park Plaza in downtown Boston, Tex slips my negligee strap down my shoulder and kisses my freckles. "Husband," I say, and she replies, "Wife." In the morning, she tells me she hardly slept because every time she remembered we'd just gotten hitched, she couldn't stop grinning. It's the first time, she tells me, that she has ever been kept awake by joy.

AUTO-COMPLETE

M. Marie

I set my chipped mug of tea down on the corner of the desk
before dropping into the chair with a soft sigh. The warm
leather squeaked against my bare thighs, and I squirmed a bit
in discomfort. It wasn't a sensation I enjoyed, but after finally
getting home from work and stripping down to my T-shirt and
panties, the thought of putting my pants back on was even less
inviting. I shifted around in search of a more comfortable position and reminded myself that I would only be sitting for a few
minutes.

In all honesty, after spending most of the day in front of a
computer screen at work, I was loath to so much as step foot
inside my girlfriend's office, but I knew our discussion from last
night would rise up again over dinner. I had resigned myself to
at least making an attempt at researching my arguments before
I had to present them again. It was tedious work, but spending
ten minutes gathering information on Google was definitely
preferable to spending another evening arguing fruitlessly with
Dahlia.

Focusing my attention on my task, I pressed the power button on the monitor and jiggled the mouse. As the dormant computer slowly pulled itself out of sleep mode, I leaned back in Dahl's leather executive chair, kicked my slippers off under the desk and pulled my feet up onto the seat. I wouldn't dare put my feet on the furniture when my girlfriend was home, but I was much more lax about the house rules when she wasn't present. Relaxing back into the soft black leather as best I could, I stifled a yawn as her fish tank screensaver finally faded into Google's homepage. It had been a long day and I was eager to spend the night curled up on the couch playing video games, but other priorities had to be attended to first.

My heart was set on spending our first-year anniversary being pampered and fussed over at the Aqua Lounge, a private adults-only spa and lounge a friend had recommended, but Dahlia was being unusually resistant. Jessika had stressed that the venue catered exclusively to lesbian couples one day a week, but my girlfriend still seemed put off by the idea that the location normally served as a meeting place for sexually adventurous single men and women.

Hoping to find some testimonials or reviews online to ease Dahlia's reservations, I clicked on the Google search box and began to enter my query: *Toronto Lesbian Spa*. As I was typing, Google's drop-down menu offered a list of possible phrases to quicken my search, as it usually did. All the suggestions were searches that had been performed recently on the same machine, so I was shocked to see the suggestion it made as I finished typing my search term.

Auto-complete, thinking my phrase *Toronto Lesbian Spa* was incomplete, was recommending I research based on an earlier enquiry: *Toronto Lesbian Spanking*.

Perplexed, I stared at the words a long moment before curiosity made me click my mouse to accept the suggested search term and bring up the results. A list of web pages related to the phrase came up instantly. I scanned through them; all of the links were blue, indicating that they had not been visited recently, but my curiosity refused to be placated by such a small fact.

I pulled up the browser's search history, not realizing I was holding my breath until it came out in an audible gasp. The list of recently visited sites painted a picture of my girlfriend that completely contradicted the intelligent, professional and charmingly feminine woman I had fallen in love with a year ago.

Scrolling through the long list of results, I clicked a number of them at random and stared in a mixture of confusion and disbelief at the web pages that opened up. Young nude women displayed themselves in a number of provocative poses, but three central themes were present in every photograph: the models all posed in ways that showcased their naked backsides, they were all teary-eyed and every single girl's bare behind was a bright, blazing red.

In some photo sets, the girl's partner was shown as well. The majority of these spankers were women. High heels, black leather and strict body language seemed to be the common components in the makeup of these disciplinarians.

My thoughts turned to Dahlia. She was a tall, beautiful woman, of visible East Indian heritage. She had long, dark hair that I loved to run my fingers through, satiny coffee-colored skin and striking eyes. She worked for the Ministry of Municipal Affairs and Housing and was passionate about the issues that crossed her desk.

This image of her that I called to mind seemed completely at odds with the girls represented in these websites.

I scrolled again through the search results, frowning. I wasn't averse to spanking itself—the activity had always piqued my aroused interest in the past—but I had never felt comfortable enough with my previous partners to broach the subject. Now that I had discovered my current lover's apparent interest in the act, however, I found myself conflicted. I had always imagined, in my private fantasies and quiet daydreams, that I would be on the receiving end if Dahl and I ever engaged in this type of play in the bedroom. The idea of Dahlia submitting to me didn't appeal to me in the slightest, regardless of the context. I wanted to make Dahlia happy, though, so I felt somewhat obligated to at least attempt this type of scene for her.

I don't know how long I sat at the computer desk silently considering the issue before Dahlia came home. All I know is that as soon as I heard her key sliding into the lock, I sprang up from the desk chair in an explosion of nervous energy. Leaving my slippers and mug behind, I fled from the room with such a guilty conscience, I wasn't surprised at all when, two minutes later, I looked up from the magazine I was desperately trying to hide behind to see my girlfriend giving me a suspicious look from the doorway of the living room.

"What did you do, Marie?"

Her question was only superficially stern; a hint of laughter colored my name as she spoke it, and I could see curious amusement softening her tired face.

With my confidence still shaken by the possible implications of my earlier discovery, however, I kept my guard up as I cautiously replied, "Nothing. I'm just reading."

One of Dahlia's dark eyebrows arched over her charcoal eyes. She wasn't used to such docile, straightforward answers from me. I cringed as she stepped across the room's threshold and approached my chair. "Really?" Her voice held a patronizing tone and my earlier uneasiness was instantly consumed by affronted petulance.

With a childish snort, I waved the magazine at her and retorted, "See?"

This was the type of response she was accustomed to. Her triumphant grin alerted me to her intentions a mere heartbeat too late; Dahlia snatched the folded magazine out of my hands and, ignoring my squawk of protest, held it just out of my reach as she asked, "Which article were you reading?"

Her smile was far too smug. I glared at her a long moment while my mind skimmed desperately through my short-term memories, searching for any phrase or key word that might have been retained from the quick glance I had made of the magazine's centerfold when I first opened it. The only words coming to mind were the ones I had recently seen displayed on Dahlia's monitor. My face flushed immediately, and, misunderstanding the cause, my girlfriend's smirk grew wider.

Scrambling for an explanation to salvage my pretence and upset her imminent victory, I blurted out, "I was researching spas!"

"In a *Canadian Living* magazine?"

Realizing that my fake alibi had been effortlessly exposed, I tried a select version of the truth. "No, I was looking them up on your computer, but," my voice faltered for a moment as I recalled the true outcome of my search, but I recovered myself quickly and continued, "but I didn't find what I expected, so I logged off."

Dahlia was standing right beside my armchair by this point, and her dark eyes were focused firmly on me as she clarified, "You couldn't find any information about day spas on the Internet? Really?"

Her facial expression and body language silently conveyed her doubt; her rich voice easily communicated her disbelief. Despite her obvious justification for the comment, I felt my temper flare up at her tone. Seeing the scowl beginning to cross my face, Dahlia sighed loudly and stepped back, shaking her head.

"I had a rough day, Marie. I don't want to pick a fight with you, okay?" Turning her back, she moved toward the doorway and I suddenly found myself on my feet, clutching the back of her suit jacket. Lifting the dark fabric, I pulled back my other hand, then brought it forward with all of my strength. My open palm smacked against the back of Dahlia's skirt. The loud sound in the quiet room made us both jump in surprise, but I masked my inexperienced reaction by boldly rebuking her: "Don't you walk away from me, little girl."

Dahlia's reaction was immediate and unanticipated.

Spinning on her heels, she slammed me back into my chair with a fierce, outraged glare. "What do you think you're doing?!" Her eyes snapped with anger and each word was bitten off carefully. I could hear in the slight trembling of her voice that she was struggling to maintain a tight control on her temper, and an unexpected and abhorrently inappropriate spark of arousal ignited inside my body. I pressed my bare legs together tightly and tried to focus my eyes on the unattractive way her nostrils were flaring rather than on the exciting way the tendons in her throat stood out when she was really livid. I could see her pulse thundering under her tan skin, and the urge to press my lips to that pressure point was dangerously strong.

This was certainly not the time, though. Dropping my gaze, I stared down at my lap while I tried to assess the volatile situation. The intensity of Dahlia's anger scared me, not for my own safety, but for the well-being of our relationship. The evidence had seemed so cut and dried. I couldn't understand where I had gone wrong in my analysis, and expressed as much when I murmured quietly, "I thought you would be into it."

Dahlia was silent. When I braved a glance up at her, I discovered she was staring down at me with an unreadable expression. I fidgeted under her steady gaze before my combined discomfort and confusion forced me to confess to her. "When I was on the computer I saw what you've been looking at. The spanking sites."

Her expression remained stony, so I implicated myself further with more admissions. "I went through your search history. I know you're interested in that kind of thing. You could have just told me, you know," I added, my tone carrying a delicate stroke of reprimand. "I'm curious about that stuff too, and even though I'm not totally comfortable with the 'spanker' role, I'm willing to try it for you."

This time when I met her gaze, Dahlia's eyes had softened. "Are you saying..." She paused for a second, and suddenly an incredulous laugh escaped her lips. "Did you really think that I wanted you to spank me? That that was my secret fantasy?"

I frowned. "What else should I think? I saw the sites you visited."

"That's true. I did visit those sites," she admitted as she stepped closer and perched on the arm of my chair. A hint of a dark smile turned up the corners of her full lips as she leaned closer and whispered in her softly accented voice, "But not for the reason you think."

She suddenly gripped my upper arm and pulled sharply. I was pulled up out of my seat just as she slid down into it. Her grip was still tight on my arm so that the twisted motion dropped me back down into the chair on top of her lap. While I was still dazed, she had no problem pulling me off balance and across her knees.

I realized immediately what was about to happen but didn't let my excitement show until I heard Dahlia's silky voice whisper, "I want to spank you."

I gasped before the first strike even landed. Dahlia wasted no effort on practice spanks. As soon as she had me pinned and recognized the eager note in my cries, she set her actions to an exhilarating, stinging pace. Her hand descended in quick, steady blows against the rounded curves of my backside. Each time her hand made a connection with my panty-covered rump, it was slightly below the previous point of contact. Within mere minutes my entire backside had been consistently slapped, and the steadily increasing heat was spreading between my legs with each additional, overlapping strike as she moved her focus back to the top of my ass to resume her play.

Her hand never stilled. I cried and squirmed, but my lover continued to firmly slap my backside. Her blows may not have been as hard as she was capable of giving, but the frequency and sheer volume was already making my rear unbelievably sore. My thin cotton panties were offering no protection at all. My legs kicked of their own accord as she moved lower to bring her hand against the sensitive place where my thighs met my ass, and I cried out in arousal and agony.

I begged now, but not for her to stop. As she finished a fifth, then sixth lap around the full surface of my behind, I spread my legs wide and pleaded with her to focus her attention lower. My pussy was dripping wet and my backside could not withstand any more of her attention.

She ignored my request at first. Her strict hand continued its silent lesson against my plump flesh, and my cries grew more frantic and desperate. Finally, reaching the thighs again, her hand lifted away from my offered ass after its most recent strike but did not immediately crash back down again.

Instead, I felt her fingers slip under the elastic waistband of my panties and slowly begin to pull the fabric down. The wetness between my legs had soaked through the cotton. As she pulled the garment down over my sore backside and exposed my damp pussy, the coolness of the air made me shudder and gasp. Ignoring me, she continued to slide my panties down my thighs, past my knees, and then off completely.

I held my breath. I lifted my rump, and to my explosive relief her fingers found my pussy and thrust deep.

My climax was quick and consuming. I screamed louder as she fucked me than I had when she spanked me, although the pleasure of one was a direct result of the pain of the other. Bucking my hips and sobbing aloud, I thrust myself back onto her slender fingers until my body couldn't tolerate any more stimulation. Then, shuddering and trembling, I released all control of my body and let myself fall limp over Dahlia's knees.

She chuckled as she pulled me back up into her lap, kissing my neck and smoothing my damp, short hair away from my face. I let her fold her arms around me and lost myself in her warm embrace until a soft rumbling from within drew my thoughts and focus back to the present.

"I'm hungry," I murmured into Dahlia's chest. I felt her laughter vibrate through her breast as she replied, "Oh, are you?"

I nodded into her blouse and sleepily demanded, "I want pizza."

"Pizza?" Dahlia reached under my chin to lift my gaze to meet hers. "You just confessed to snooping through my computer, Marie! Do you honestly think you deserve takeout tonight?"

A bold grin was my only reply.

"Brat!" she scolded, and reached down to land a playful slap on my already aching ass. I gasped and gave her an outraged look, but she didn't notice it. Her attention was already diverted to searching for the cordless phone under the small stack of magazines on the coffee table beside our chair.

THE INSATIABLE TRAVEL ITCH

Evan Mora

S he might touch my hand. She might lace her fingers through mine.

"Hey, baby..." she might begin. Honey. Babe. Universal endearments.

I could wrap my arm around her waist, kiss her silly in broad daylight, grind my pussy into her cock in a crowded club full of dykes; I could make her my wife.

We take this for granted—our privilege—how can we not? The biggest parade in the city celebrates us. One million people cheering and waving flags.

But.

Transported, transplanted, we are transgressors. And it makes me fucking wet.

It starts when we get on the plane. We shuffle down the aisle with a smattering of murmured apologies, too many people in too small a space all trying to do the same things simultaneously. We are three to a side, me in the window, Dale in the middle, and a stranger on the aisle, the three of us intimately sandwiched together so that even our whispers are shared.

I want to kiss her, but I don't. Who is this woman sitting next to her? Dale no more wants to sit in the middle than I do, but her tolerance for banal pleasantries is greater than mine, and she trades thoughts on the weather and vacation details with this woman whose name we'll never know, despite five hours spent with knees touching and the fact that our trips to the bathroom rely on her goodwill.

Dale's inclined slightly toward this woman, which means her back is to me. I want to slide my hand beneath her shirt and feel the warmth of her skin. I want to travel lazy fingertips up her spine and trace patterns across her back with my nails. I don't do these things, and the want becomes a slow burn, born of denial, that takes up residence somewhere deep inside me.

I am not, in general, overly enamored with public displays of affection, so the irony of this situation is not lost on me. We seldom even hold hands when we're out, and yet here, where I feel we *should* be more circumspect, I want to be anything but.

This woman could be anyone—though the presence of a man with a matching ring on the opposite aisle tells me clearly that she's not gay. How would she react if I leaned across Dale's lap and kissed her full on the mouth? If I curled my hands into Dale's sweater and slid my tongue between her parted lips? Would she look at us with disgust?

"You're a freak," Dale teases me, accustomed to this curious phenomenon, and the happy object of my ravenous vacation desires.

"Hmph." I shrug with feigned indifference, passing the time with a novel, my iPod and stale reruns of *Friends*, filthy daydreams of Dale's fist in my cunt playing themselves out to their wet, nasty conclusions in my mind, arousal simmering pleasantly in my nether parts.

We arrive with little fanfare on this tiny Caribbean island of thirty thousand souls, descending the staircase wheeled out to greet our arrival and walking across the blistering-hot tarmac in our long pants, heading toward a single door that says *Arrivals*. A fan whirls ineffectually overhead while efficient men in official-looking uniforms sit in tiny air-conditioned booths inspecting our passports.

"You're traveling together?" says our man, perusing our immigration documents.

"Yes," we reply. I wonder if he notes our shared address?

"What's the purpose of your visit?" he asks, gaze shifting from Dale's face to mine impassively, and I feel a small thrill, thinking of the box I checked, the one marked *pleasure*.

"Vacation," Dale answers. He seems satisfied.

We secure our luggage and head to the next cluster of officials; customs always raises my pulse a little, even though I haven't had the courage to keep the bag of cocks and vibrators and condoms and lube in my suitcase, tucking them instead in the bottom of Dale's bag next to her mask and fins. The last time we traveled they searched her suitcase as I stood next to her on trembling legs, fear and arousal beating through me in alternating pulses. Would they open the bag? Would they reach inside? Pull out the fat cock still attached to her harness? Lay it on the table for countless eyes to see? As it happened, they didn't even glance at the small bag, presuming I guess that it was snorkeling gear like all the rest, all of my imaginings much ado about nothing.

This time we're waved through, and we collect our rental car and drive to our destination without incident. Generous friends have given us the use of their two-bedroom condo in a quiet seaside complex we'd fallen in love with a year ago. We're greeted by the same woman that greeted us the last time we were here, and we collect our keys amiably as she gives the standard spiel about where to park and which keys unlock which doors.

I wonder if she remembers us? Dale with her short messy hair, her baseball cap and boy shorts, and me with my long wavy hair, painted toes and tiny, girly bikinis? We who don't conform to the image of a couple of girlfriends away on vacation while our husbands go golfing back home; we who obviously aren't sisters...

"You care too much about what other people think," Dale says.

I do; I know. I want to please everyone. And so I'm careful to call her by her name instead of any of the slew of endearments I'd use at home; I'm careful not to touch her when we're lying side by side on our loungers in the hot afternoon sun. But I think about it constantly and get more and more aroused—I can't help myself. And I imagine that everyone around us knows, and that they call us perverts and deviants in their minds even as they smile politely and make small talk.

By the end of the day I'm aching to feel her pressed against me, and we've scarcely closed the door before I'm climbing on top of her, fusing my mouth to hers in the center of the king-sized bed, despite the fact that the bellboy has pointedly left our luggage at the ends of the two twin beds in the other bedroom.

There's a break in the kissing and I'm fumbling with the ties on my bikini, tearing it off with a curse and flinging it to the ground while Dale efficiently removes her clothes, chuckling at my urgency. I push her by the shoulders and she tumbles backward obligingly. I settle on top of her, grinding my slick pussy into her thigh, smearing salt and sunblock and my own arousal together.

I think briefly of the bag of toys tucked in the suitcase in the other room, about how much I love the feel of Dale's cock driving deep inside me, but that's not what I need right now. Dale knows it too, and tangles one hand in my long hair, drawing me down for a kiss that is soft lips and the wet slide of tongues. She slides her other hand down my back, urging me closer to her, until no space separates the feminine contours of our bodies. I revel in the feel of her breasts pressed against mine, our nipples hard and straining together; I moan at the downy soft feel of her belly touching mine.

Her hand trails lower, coming to rest on the generous curve of my ass, gripping me there as she raises her leg slightly, sliding me forward into the saddle between her hip bone and thigh, holding me tight as I ride her, her arousal wet against my thigh and the rich musky scent of our mingled desire thick in the air.

There is no cock, real or silicone, in this room right now, and although I know Dale feels more comfortable with her cock than without it, she gives me this—this moment of pure, unabashed girl on girl, and it makes me wetter than ever. All the blood in my body races to my clit when she sucks on my tongue and I moan, cupping her breast in my hand as I rock against her. Her thigh is slippery with my juices and I grind my clit against her slick skin until orgasm races down my spine.

The next day is more of the same. I can't get it out of my system. We walk through the port town surrounded by couples holding hands, a gulf of careful distance screaming between us, and my fingers itch with the need to touch, flexing at my side and curling into fists of self-denial. I want to lick the salt from her neck and rub myself up against her like a cat. I want to mark her as mine.

"Would you take our picture?" A sunburnt woman smiles at me, gesturing to a sunburnt man at her side.

"Sure," I say, watching them in the LCD display, his arm

around her shoulder, her arm around his waist, two red noses touching with a secret shared smile against the backdrop of the brilliant turquoise sea.

"Ready?" I say, and they flash me their smiles.

Honeymoons. Anniversaries. Romantic getaways. The space between Dale and me is thrown into relief by the abundance of affection on display around us, and I feel a recklessness tingling in me as I imagine straddling Dale's lap on a bench in the middle of town, stripping off my shirt and feeding her my breasts. A tiny sound escapes my lips and Dale smiles at me wolfishly. She doesn't need to hear my thoughts to know what I'm thinking and she takes full advantage of my arousal, whispering all manner of dirty things in my ear under the guise of pointing things out in shop windows.

She's got me so wet I'm practically panting and rational thought is rapidly disappearing. Right now I'd be happy in a public bathroom with Dale tonguing my clit—hell, I'd settle for a blanket thrown over my lap in the car and Dale's fingers pumping into me.

"Come on—I know someplace we can go," she says, leading us through the crowds and back to the car.

For a moment I think she's had the same idea that I have, but her hands stay on the wheel and she guides us out of town and into the countryside. We travel for maybe ten or fifteen minutes, pavement giving way to dirt roads, and finally to two narrow tracks cutting across field and brush. I know where she's taken us, and my pussy thrums with anticipation—it's a deserted beach we discovered last year, the site of an old resort that had been destroyed a decade ago by a passing hurricane. Only some footings remained, barely visible now beneath the encroaching scrub and brush. We'd explored this place last year with our friends and hadn't seen another soul the entire afternoon.

"Baby, you're brilliant!" I exclaim with delight, ditching my seat belt and inching as close to her as I can as we travel the last few hundred yards through the brush. I nibble on her earlobe and press my breasts against her arm, slide my hand up her thigh.

"I thought you'd like this," she says with a smile. "Why don't you grab us a couple of towels?"

I lean between the seats and rummage in our bag, triumphantly producing two towels just as Dale pulls into the clearing and stops the car with a curse.

"What is it?" I ask, but a quick glance tells me all I need to know.

There's another car parked a few feet in front of us and a guy and a girl making out on the beach. We cut the engine and sit in silence.

"What do we do now?" I ask.

"We wait 'em out," she says, wicked promise in her eyes. "Come on."

We get out of the car and head off down the beach in the opposite direction. We walk as far as we can, then turn and head back, but instead of leaving, the couple has gone swimming.

"Great." I pout.

"They can't swim forever," Dale says.

They can't, it's true. In fact, they're really not even swimming now—they're locked in an embrace again, her arms around his neck, their mouths fused together, rocking together slowly in the chest-deep water.

"You don't think they're..." But my sentence trails off. They're fucking. No doubt about it.

I don't know what I feel. It's like I've been pushed over some critical edge I didn't know I was skirting. Screw discretion—I want to tear off my clothes and spread my pussy open and have Dale go down on me right there on the beach.

"Uh-oh," Dale says, eyeing my expression and hurriedly scanning the area.

"Come on," she says, heading quickly down the beach once more while I follow, my pulse deafening in my ears, blood roaring through me, swelling my pussy, pulsing in my clit.

Dale picks up an overgrown footpath leading into the bushes, tromping inland with the stealth of an elephant and a string of muttered curses as I stalk behind her like a hungry predator. When I reach her she's in a makeshift clearing, towels spread on the ground.

I kiss her hard, but really, I don't have much patience for preliminaries right now and we go from upright to horizontal without much grace, and I'm pulling my bikini bottom to one side and Dale's mouth is finally, gloriously, on my pussy. She laps up my juices and latches on to my clit, forgoing any teasing in favor of sucking and tonguing me with a rhythm that always makes me come.

"More!" I growl at her and she complies by thrusting three fingers deep in my pussy, pumping me as she works my clit. It's still not enough, though, and I push her head away, stroking my clit furiously as she fucks me all the harder, wet sloppy sounds accompanying my grunts and pants, my stomach muscles clenched so tight I think they're going to snap. And then the dam bursts, and I'm gushing around her fingers, engulfed in waves of release, crying out my joy.

A minute passes, maybe two. Dale sits up as I lie there trying to catch my breath, shaking her hand and wincing a little.

"I swear you're going to break my fingers one of these days." She rubs her neck like it's sore too, then gets slowly to her feet, brushing the sand from her shins.

As my higher brain functions return, it occurs to me that there's some kind of stick or root digging into my back and a fine layer of sand pretty much...everywhere. I climb gingerly to my feet, rubbing my back with a wince of my own.

"So...sex on the beach...everything you imagined?" Dale deadpans. We laugh a little at the picture we must make, a couple of dykes getting it on in the bush.

"We could have just left," I offer.

"Uh-uh." Dale shakes her head. "I know what's good for me. You're scary when you don't get laid."

"Oh, ha ha. Very funny."

"Whatever. You want to get out of here?" she says, shaking out our towels.

"Do you think those people heard us?" I ask, suddenly feeling a little self-conscious.

"I don't know, that was quite the war cry you let out." Dale smirks.

There's really nothing to do but make our way back, so we do, and I breathe a little sigh of relief when I see that ours is the only car left on the beach. The sun is getting low in the sky, and Dale holds my hand as we cruise along in our little blue car. She's got some nasty-looking scratches on her shins from the thorns in the underbrush and I think a little sheepishly that she's gotten the fuzzy end of the lollipop today—a wrong I'm determined to right.

We grab some takeout and head back to the condo, losing the sand-filled swimsuits and showering off before slipping into something more comfortable. We open a bottle of wine and throw open the doors, enjoying a leisurely meal on the ground-level terrace. It's dark now, and while we can't see the water anymore, the view is still spectacular. The twinkling lights of private villas dot the rugged hillside opposite us, and the muted sounds of reggae drift on the breeze. We're only a little way away from the strip of beach bars that fills with locals and tourists nearly every night, and while I can't see them, I can hear the laughter of the people who make their way there, walking along the darkened road in front of our complex.

We are illuminated by the terrace light, and I wonder if any of those people look up at Dale and me. I wonder if they can see us clearly. I touch Dale's thigh experimentally and feel a corresponding tingle run through me. Emboldened, I lean forward and press my lips to hers, my tongue sweeping into her mouth for a fleeting moment, barely touching hers before retreating. I lean back in my chair, looking out into the night once more and listening to the sounds, but nothing has changed and arousal swirls low in my belly as I contemplate the myriad of possibilities.

"Dirty girl," Dale says to me, but her eyes are hungry and a seductive smile teases my lips.

I angle my chair closer to hers and my hand is on her thigh. Resting. Stroking. Inching higher. We sip our wine in silence and gaze into the darkness, our casualness betrayed by erratic breathing. Her hand settles on top of mine, guiding me upward until I'm cupping the shaft she's concealed beneath her shorts. My eyes widen in surprise.

"When did you—"

"When we got back."

That fast I'm wet again. I stroke her lightly through the thin cotton and her eyes close with pleasure. I unzip her fly and slide my hand inside, wrap her cock in my fist. I take my time, working her slowly, teasing a low groan from her parted lips.

"Oh baby, that's nice..." she murmurs, and I squeeze her shaft a little harder, feel her hips rise as she thrusts into my palm.

"You like that?" I tease, leaning in to place a kiss on her jaw, dancing out of reach before her lips can capture mine.

"You know I do." Her voice is husky with desire and I know she wants more, but I don't increase my pace, stroking her with maddening slowness.

There's a shout from somewhere in the darkness and my heart slams in my chest, but an answering shout followed by laughter allays my fear, and the sound drifts gradually away. The shot of adrenaline goes straight to my clit, arousing me all the more.

"You *are* a dirty girl," Dale growls in my ear, nipping my earlobe before leaning back in her seat once more.

I slide my hand out of her shorts and move so that I'm sitting with one foot on the back of her chair and the other on her knee, giving her a wide-open view of my crotch, covered only by the thin strip of chocolate-brown terry cloth on my barely-there shorts.

"What makes you say that?" I feign innocence, sipping my wine and looking casually out into the night.

"This," she says, and slips a finger beneath the fabric, running it along my wet slit. She circles my clit teasingly, then dips inside, first one, then two fingers fucking me with the same aching slowness that I stroked her with moments ago. It's deliciously sublime, and I can't help but moan, my legs spread wide, the warm breeze kissing my exposed flesh, Dale's fingers exploring my depths.

I could stay like that forever, but I'm losing my focus and I know my girl is hungry, so I reluctantly lower my legs and Dale slides out of me. She starts to raise her fingers to her mouth, but I beat her to it, capturing her wrist and licking my juices from her, sucking her fingers like I want to suck her cock.

"Oh Jesus..." she says, and I let her taste me then, her tongue sweeping into my mouth, capturing my essence.

I break the kiss and whisper in her ear, ask her if she wants my mouth on her cock. She unbuttons her shorts and palms her shaft, stroking it the way that only she can, watching me as I watch her jerk off, knowing it gets me off like nothing else. She grips it near the base and my lips sink over her head and down her shaft until they kiss her knuckles.

"Fuck yes, baby..." she groans, and I do it again, my mouth rising and falling on her cock. I love the weight of her on my tongue; I love the thickness that stretches my mouth wide. I lose myself in sucking her off, in the rhythmic motion of my head and her hips, which rise helplessly each time my mouth descends.

"Inside," she finally says, grabbing her shorts and my hand, pulling me into our bedroom and closing the door.

Her mouth is fierce on my swollen lips, her tongue thrusting deeply, urgently against mine. Our clothes disappear and I'm pinned beneath her, in the center of that king-sized bed once more. We kiss with a frenzied hunger, and her hand is between us, testing my readiness, guiding her cock into me. She sinks into my pussy until she can go no further, until I am blissfully, achingly full. I want to ride that sensation but I've stoked a raging fire in her and she pumps into me, rocking the bed with the force of her thrusts.

I'm a slut for her cock, spread as wide as I can, my hands on her ass, holding her tight. Our bodies are slick and heaving together, our kisses interspersed with grunts and moans. She fucks me to get herself off and I love it. She doesn't worry about me; she knows she doesn't have to. I get off on feeling her slip over that edge; sometimes I swear I can feel her coming inside me.

I know she's right there; I feel the tension in her muscles, hear the change in her breathing that tells me she's close. My legs start to tremble and my fingers dig into her skin, my pussy clenches around her cock as her hips jerk forward, propelled by the orgasm that's tearing through her and then into me. It goes on forever between her body and mine, pushed beyond rational limits by the momentum we generate.

We're spent and exhausted and she collapses next to me. I hold her hand and we stare at the ceiling, chests heaving as we try to find enough air. I'm dying for some water, but I feel like I'm glued to the sheets. I'm not sure I could get up even if I tried.

"Again?" Dale says and we laugh, endorphins buzzing happily in our brains.

I am at ease, within and without, content to sink into a languorous stupor with her, here in this private space where we are free to do as we please.

"Hey, baby—" she says, and I am profoundly happy, kissing the rest of her words away.

The next morning we decide to do breakfast at a local cafe that has fabulous views out over the Caribbean. We chat quietly over coffee while we wait for our meal, laughing softly between ourselves.

"Are you guys sisters?" our waiter asks, his expression speculative as he tries to put his finger on that intangible familiarity between us.

"No," I say, and I feel it start all over again. I want to tell him we're lovers. I want to lean over and kiss her beautiful mouth and show him exactly what kind of relationship we have. I want to tell him she's the best fuck I've ever had. I want...

Dale's looking at me, trying unsuccessfully to hide a smile. We've still got five more days to go. Damn, I love vacation.

ABOUT THE AUTHORS

CHEYENNE BLUE's (www.cheyenneblue.com) erotica has appeared in over 60 anthologies including *Best Women's Erotica, Mammoth Best New Erotica, Cowboy Lust: Erotic Romance for Women* and *Lesbian Cops*. She trained as a nurse in London, but nowadays tries to restrict her "nursing" to raising blood pressure and pulse.

CHARLOTTE DARE's erotic fiction has appeared in *The Harder She Comes: Butch Femme Erotica, Best Lesbian Romance, Best Lesbian Erotica, Lesbian Cowboys, Girl Crazy, Ultimate Lesbian Erotica, Wetter: More True Lesbian Sex Stories, Where the Girls Are* and various online publications. She thanks her red-hot lover, Ana, for her endless inspiration.

JASMINE GRIMSTEAD is an educator, a graduate student and an advocate for LGBT youth. She does her working and playing in North Carolina, where you can find her enjoying the mountains or writing erotica in her free time.

CATHERINE HENREID lives in Berlin, but her heart is still in Israel. She would never admit to being a Polonia. Her work has appeared in Silver Publishing's Dreaming of a White Christmas series.

H.M. HUSLEY is a writer, storyteller and artist. Constantly seeking out new adventures and experiences, lesbian erotica is just one of her methods of expression. She is inspired by Anaïs Nin, Oscar Wilde and joie de vivre. She is based in St. Paul, Minnesota.

LYNETTE MAE served in the army before diving into a law enforcement career. Her life's rich experiences provide endless inspiration for stories filled with real-life action and plenty of romance. LM's characters, like the author, never settle for the ordinary. What's next from the mind of Lynette Mae? Stand by.

M. MARIE (www.mmarie.ca) lives in the heart of downtown Toronto. This passionate young Canadian is soft-spoken, inquisitive and addicted to art, opera, writing and video games. Having previously won several writers' awards for her poetry and short stories, she is excited to now be branching out into erotic publications.

DAWN MCKAY is a self-admitted recluse who spent the better part of her military career under "Don't Ask, Don't Tell." Eight months before retirement she saw it lifted. With a light heart she was able to set aside decades of battles for equal rights and retire back to Texas.

DANIELLE MIGNON is a lover of live theater and photography who's been called a grammar geek and control freak. An editor of countless stories, she's moving to the foreground by putting pen to paper. Ms. Mignon is a country girl with city tastes and a unique outlook on life.

ALLISON MOON is the author of the lesbian werewolf novel *Lunatic Fringe*, nominated for a 2011 Golden Crown Award. The sequel, *Hungry Ghost*, was released in Spring 2013. A popular speaker and educator, Allison teaches workshops on creativity, art, writing, social justice and sexuality. Find out more at her website TalesofthePack.com.

DESTINY MOON is a shy and bookish femme who, when she isn't wooing sexy butches, spends a lot of time nerding out in her apartment. She would like to dedicate her story to the pornographer, the source of her inspiration. Visit Destiny's blog at http://eroticauthoress.blogspot.ca/.

EVAN MORA loves traveling, long walks on the beach and writing about all sorts of sexy things. Find her in anthologies like: *Best Lesbian Erotica '09* & *'12*, *Best Lesbian Romance '09*, *'10* & *'12*, *Lesbian Cops*, *Girl Fever* and *The Harder She Comes: Butch/Femme Erotica*. She lives in Toronto.

MONICA E. MORENO was born and raised in the Southwestern United States. She is the writer of Chicana-themed romance/erotica, poetry and literary fiction. During the day she works as a secretary, and at night she practices *recetas* passed down through her family. She still believes in *los cuentos de hadas* she heard growing up.

DAWN MUELLER is the author of the recently published memoir *A Single Year*. She lives on the north side of Chicago with her chocolate lab, Mousse, and her incorrigible kitten, Kazoo. She writes about lesbians, sex and relationships and, thankfully, remembers it all the next morning.

CATHERINE PAULSSEN's (www.catherinepaulssen.com) stories have appeared in *Best Lesbian Romance 2012* and *Girl Fever* and in anthologies by Ravenous Romance and Constable & Robinson.

ANGEL PROPPS is a femme leatherdyke, collared submissive, Ms. SouthEastLeatherFest 2011, First Runner-up International Ms. Leather 2012, multi-published writer of erotica and horror and poetry who spends her time traveling the country with her whip-vending Daddy. They both can be found at various conferences presenting classes and playing in dungeons.

Eroticist **GISELLE RENARDE** (www.wix.com/gisellerenarde/erotica) is a queer Canadian, avid volunteer, contributor to more than 50 short story anthologies and author of dozens of electronic and print books, including *Anonymous*, *Ondine* and *My Mistress' Thighs*. Ms. Renarde lives across from a park with two bilingual cats who sleep on her head.

MIA SAVAGE, when she's not working as a graphic designer and award-winning photographer, dons heavy black horn-rimmed glasses and sexy lingerie in which to write contemporary lesbian erotica. Her lusty tales and micro poetry have been featured in the online Erotica Gallery of the Erotica Readers and Writers Association.

ANNA WATSON remembers the days when a nice suburban femme like herself would have had a very difficult time finding a place to hook up with fine butches like the ones mentioned here. She dedicates this story to butch-femme.com, where she had such very good luck, and to her husband, SD.

ALLISON WONDERLAND (aisforallison.blogspot.com) is one L of a girl. In college, she studied dramatic writing, women and women's studies. In addition to storytelling, Allison enjoys theater, glitz and grammar. Her lesbian literature appears in *Girl Fever, Sapphic Planet, Milk and Honey, Bound by Lust* and *Girls Who Score.*

ABOUT
THE EDITOR

SACCHI GREEN is a Lambda Award–winning writer and editor of erotica and other stimulating genres. Her stories have appeared in scores of publications, including seven volumes of *Best Lesbian Erotica*, four of *Best Women's Erotica* and four of *Best Lesbian Romance*. In recent years she's taken to wielding the editorial whip, editing eight lesbian erotica anthologies, most recently *Lesbian Cowboys* (winner of a Lambda Literary Award in 2010), *Girl Crazy*, *Lesbian Lust*, *Lesbian Cops* and *Girl Fever: 69 Stories of Sudden Sex for Lesbians*, all from Cleis Press. Sacchi lives in the Five College area of western Massachusetts, with frequent trips to the White Mountains of New Hampshire, and can be found online at sacchi-green.blogspot.com, FaceBook (as Sacchi Green) and Live Journal (as sacchig).

More from Sacchi Green

Girl Fever
69 Stories of Sudden Sex for Lesbians
Edited by Sacchi Green

This big book of lesbian quickies, with stories from top-notch contributors, evokes the heat, urgency and "gotta have it" moments of sudden sex. There are long-time companions, one-night stands, meet-cutes and meet-only-once stories to fuel every fantasy.
ISBN 978-1-57344-791-1 $15.95

Lesbian Cops
Erotic Investigations
Edited by Sacchi Green

What is it about lesbian cops that push all the right buttons? The top-flight fiction writers tapped by Sacchi Green in *Lesbian Cops* capture that irresistible force—and channel it into fiercely erotic stories.
ISBN 978-1-57344-651-8 $14.95

Lesbian Lust
Erotic Stories
Edited by Sacchi Green

"Lust: It's the engine that drives us wild on the way to getting us off, and lesbian lust is the heart, soul and red-hot core of this anthology."—Sacchi Green, from the Introduction
ISBN 978-1-57344-403-3 $14.95

Lesbian Cowboys
Erotic Adventures
Edited by Sacchi Green and Rakelle Valencia

With stories that are edgy as shiny spurs and tender as broken-in leather, fifteen first-rate writers share their take on cowboys—the iconic fantasy, the calling, and the attitude that has nothing to do with gender.
ISBN 978-1-57344-361-6 $14.95

Girl Crazy
Coming Out Erotica
Edited by Sacchi Green

These irresistible stories of first times of all kinds invite the reader to savor that delicious, dizzy feeling known as "girl crazy."
ISBN 978-1-57344-352-4 $14.95

More of the Best Lesbian Erotica

Essential Lesbian Erotica

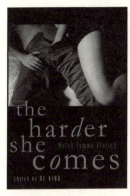

The Harder She Comes
Butch/Femme Erotica
Edited by D. L. King

Some butches worship at the altar of their femmes, and many adorable girls long for the embrace of their suave, sexy daddies. In *The Harder She Comes*, we meet femmes who salivate at the sight of packed jeans and bois who dream of touching the corseted waist of a beautiful, confident woman.
ISBN 978-1-57344-778-2 $14.95

Girls Who Bite
Lesbian Vampire Erotica
Edited by Delilah Devlin

Whether depicting a traditional blood-drinker seducing a meal, a psychic vampire stealing the life force of an unknowing host, or a real-life sanguinarian seeking a partner to share a ritual bloodletting, the stories in *Girls Who Bite* are a sensual surprise.
ISBN 978-1-57344-715-7 $14.95

Girls Who Score
Hot Lesbian Erotica
Edited by Ily Goyanes

Girl jocks always manage to see a lot of action off the field. *Girls Who Score* is a winner, filled with story after story of competitive, intriguing women engaging in all kinds of contact sports.
ISBN 978-1-57344-825-3 $15.95

She Shifters
Lesbian Paranormal Erotica
Edited by Delilah Devlin

Delilah Devlin has delved deep to find fantastic tales of love and sex that know no bounds—think *Twilight* meets *The L Word* and turn up the heat. Her untamed shapeshifters will ignite your imagination with visions of primal passions and insatiable hungers.
ISBN 978-1-57344-796-6 $15.95

Stripped Down
Lesbian Sex Stories
Edited by Tristan Taormino

Where else but in a Tristan Taormino erotica collection can you find a femme vigilante, a virgin baby butch and a snake handler jostling for attention? The salacious stories in *Stripped Down* will draw you in and sweep you off your feet.
ISBN 978-1-57344-794-2 $15.95

More of the Best Lesbian Romance

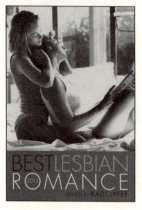

Best Lesbian Romance 2012
Edited by Radclyffe

Best Lesbian Romance 2012 celebrates the dizzying sensation of falling in love—and the electrifying thrill of sexual passion. Romance maestra Radclyffe gathers irresistible stories of lesbians in love to awaken your desire and send your imagination soaring.
ISBN 978-1-57344-757-7 $14.95

Best Lesbian Romance 2011
Edited by Radclyffe

"*Best Lesbian Romance* series editor Radclyffe has assembled a respectable crop of 17 authors for this year's offering. The stories are diverse in tone, style and subject, each containing a satisfying, surprising twist."—*Curve*
ISBN 978-1-57344-427-9 $14.95

Best Lesbian Romance 2010
Edited by Radclyffe

Ranging from the short and ever-so-sweet to the recklessly passionate, *Best Lesbian Romance 2010* is essential reading for anyone who favors the highly imaginative, the deeply sensual, and the very loving.
ISBN 978-1-57344-376-0 $14.95

Best Lesbian Romance 2009
Edited by Radclyffe

Scale the heights of emotion and the depths of desire with this collection of the very best lesbian romance writing of the year.
ISBN 978-1-57344-333-3 $14.95

Fuel Your Fantasies

Carnal Machines
Steampunk Erotica
Edited by D. L. King

In this decadent fusing of technology and romance, outstanding contemporary erotica writers use the enthralling possibilities of the 19th-century steam age to tease and titillate.
ISBN 978-1-57344-654-9 $14.95

The Sweetest Kiss
Ravishing Vampire Erotica
Edited by D. L. King

These sanguine tales give new meaning to the term "dead sexy" and feature beautiful bloodsuckers whose desires go far beyond blood.
ISBN 978-1-57344-371-5 $15.95

The Handsome Prince
Gay Erotic Romance
Edited by Neil Plakcy

A bawdy collection of bedtime stories brimming with classic fairy tale characters, reimagined and recast for any man who has dreamt of the day his prince will come. These sexy stories fuel fantasies and remind us all of the power of true romance.
ISBN 978-1-57344-659-4 $14.95

Daughters of Darkness
Lesbian Vampire Tales
Edited by Pam Keesey

"A tribute to the sexually aggressive woman and her archetypal roles, from nurturing goddess to dangerous predator."—*The Advocate*
ISBN 978-1-57344-233-6 $14.95

Dark Angels
Lesbian Vampire Erotica
Edited by Pam Keesey

Dark Angels collects tales of lesbian vampires, the quintessential bad girls, archetypes of passion and terror. These tales of desire are so sharply erotic you'll swear you've been bitten!
ISBN 978-1-57344-252-7 $13.95

Ordering is easy! Call us toll free or fax us to place your MC/VISA order.
You can also mail the order form below with payment to:
Cleis Press, 2246 Sixth St., Berkeley, CA 94710.

**Buy 4 books,
Get 1 *FREE*** *

ORDER FORM

QTY	TITLE	PRICE
⸺	⸺⸺⸺⸺⸺⸺⸺⸺⸺	⸺⸺
⸺	⸺⸺⸺⸺⸺⸺⸺⸺⸺	⸺⸺
⸺	⸺⸺⸺⸺⸺⸺⸺⸺⸺	⸺⸺
⸺	⸺⸺⸺⸺⸺⸺⸺⸺⸺	⸺⸺
⸺	⸺⸺⸺⸺⸺⸺⸺⸺⸺	⸺⸺
⸺	⸺⸺⸺⸺⸺⸺⸺⸺⸺	⸺⸺
⸺	⸺⸺⸺⸺⸺⸺⸺⸺⸺	⸺⸺

SUBTOTAL ⸺⸺

SHIPPING ⸺⸺

SALES TAX ⸺⸺

TOTAL ⸺⸺

Add $3.95 postage/handling for the first book ordered and $1.00 for each additional book. Outside North America, please contact us for shipping rates. California residents add 9% sales tax. Payment in U.S. dollars only.

* Free book of equal or lesser value. Shipping and applicable sales tax extra.

Cleis Press • Phone: (800) 780-2279 • Fax: (510) 845-8001
orders@cleispress.com • www.cleispress.com
You'll find more great books on our website

Follow us on Twitter @cleispress • Friend/fan us on Facebook